I0568012

Loch was forced to pick a member of the University of North Carolina football team to date early in his freshman year. He had taken a chance on a scrawny freshman named Marcus. Two years later, in their junior years, Marcus has blossomed into a hulking football-playing man. Loch has kept up with the man he believes is his true Master, but now they have to meet each other's families. Either their connection will remain strong or fray under the scrutiny of their loved ones. Also looming in the future is the end of their senior year. What will happen when they go their separate ways?

The unauthorized reproduction or distribution of this copyrighted work is illegal. Criminal copyright infringement, including infringement without monetary gain, is investigated by the FBI and is punishable by up to 5 years in federal prison and a fine of $250,000.

This book is a work of fiction. Names, characters, places, and incidents either are products of the author's imagination or are used fictitiously. Any resemblance to actual events or locales or persons, living or dead, is entirely coincidental.

Cageless In College Junior Year
Copyright © 2021 Crawford Rhine
ISBN: 978-1-4874-3143-3
Cover art by Martine Jardin

All rights reserved. Except for use in any review, the reproduction or utilization of this work in whole or in part in any form by any electronic, mechanical or other means, now known or hereafter invented, is forbidden without the written permission of the publisher.

Published by eXtasy Books Inc or
Devine Destinies, an imprint of eXtasy Books Inc

Look for us online at:
www.eXtasybooks.com or www.devinedestinies.com

Cageless In College Junior Year

By

Crawford Rhine

CHAPTER ONE

June had brought the end of school and the beginning of another summer in Charleston for me. I had just finished my second year at the University of North Carolina, having the most amazing sexual experience of my life.

Now I was supposed to go home for three months and live without it?

Marcus Battle had been my boyfriend since the first month of freshman year when the football team decided that I needed one of them to fuck me on a regular basis. I didn't like being told what to do, but at the same time, I was given free rein to choose any football player I wanted to date, so it was a win-win situation for me.

I was a marked man, in a literal sense. On my face was a bright blue mark running from my earlobe to my chin. The mark appeared on the exact minute of my birth on my thirteenth birthday. It signaled to the world that I was a man who was sexually attracted to men, and since our world only contained men, it was one big meat market for me.

My father had always taught me that our world contained more threats to me than pleasures and he had been correct. NOMARs, or non-marked men, made up about ninety-eight percent of the population, and since there were no women, they were constantly horny. Dad had taught me to fight and defend myself, but most importantly, he had taught me how to think quickly, react in advance, and how to quickly assess my surroundings for potential danger.

Fortunately for me, I had not run into any major problems.

Once in high school, I found a popular senior to date who usually ran interference for me and kept trouble at bay. I did the same thing the next year and then the next and assumed that I would live my life that way. These men were easy to manipulate, and most of them bent to my will without even the flicker of fight in their eyes.

When I arrived on campus at UNC, I naturally thought it would be smart to find a protector, but I also let loose a little and fucked around with a lot of guys. By the time the football team offered me their protection, I was ready to see what came of it. Dating several of the older players, I found them lacking. Fortunately for me, I was intrigued by a quiet freshman and gave him a chance.

Marcus turned out to be the most amazing man I had ever met. He was not as susceptible to my charms as every other NOMAR I had met and refused to fuck me or even let me see his cock until I had committed to him. There was some kind of attraction between the two of us that I could not explain. I had never felt anything like it before, and I could not get enough of it.

It took two weeks for me to take the risk and accept Marcus as the football player that I wanted to date. He had been there when I needed him and I told him that I wanted him to be my boyfriend. He was excited, but still held out on sex until I informed the team of my decision.

When Marcus and I finally fucked, it was mind-blowing sex that I had never felt before. Marcus' cock was huge and he certainly knew how to use it, but the real fire came from the connection between us. We just couldn't get enough of each other, and therefore we had to set limits very quickly. Marcus and I were both excellent students and he also was a member of the football team, so we didn't want either of those two things to suffer just because we couldn't stay out of each other's pants.

We spent our first year together feeling each other out. Marcus demanded that I work out to be able to keep up with him, and I was more than willing. I didn't want anything to hold me back from being with him. Marcus and I had a great year together, and over the summer, he had told me to take an older lover to keep me out of trouble.

I had worked out a deal with the boss at my summer job at IBM that allowed him to fuck around with me in exchange for a summer job and the company scholarship each school year. Mr. Lewellyn, my boss, had taught me more than I bargained for. He was into bondage, and the things that he did to me, made me realize that I wanted to explore it with Marcus.

My chance to do just that came at the end of summer when I bound myself to Marcus' locker on the last day of football camp. He took total advantage of me and we wound up spending the rest of the summer together. It was such life-altering sex, but neither Marcus nor I were ready to fully realize what it meant.

Marcus Battle had started to make some noise on the football field in his second year and we both had matured physically in the year since we had met. Marcus had grown into a man and not an overgrown boy like before.

A spring break trip in our sophomore year to the Bahamas had sealed the connection for us. We both had enjoyed someone else's attention on that trip, but had come out of the other side to realize that we were what each of us needed. I had marked him as my man and he had marked me as his.

At the end of our second year, Marcus had snatched me from my final exam and taken me to a hotel room where he asserted his dominance over me. My footballer boyfriend had bound me, controlled me, forced me to address him as Master, and then given me the greatest sexual pleasure of my life.

That experience had happened a week ago. I was now at home in Charleston, and Marcus was at his father's home in

Ohio. I thought back to it often.

After fucking for most of twelve hours, Marcus and I had collapsed on the bed, too exhausted to move. We talked instead.

Marcus asked, "Are you planning to continue fucking around with Mr. Lewellyn for the summer, Loch?"

"If you do not want me to, I will wait for you, Marcus." This was the first time since we'd arrived at the hotel room the day before that we had used each other's names.

"No, you can't wait. You know how crazy you get when you're not fucked on a regular basis."

"I can spend my summer with you and . . . get fucked on a regular basis," I said, flirting with him shamelessly.

"I wish," Marcus said with a sigh. "But you know that I have to be in Portland for most of it."

I did know that Marcus had received an opportunity to work out with some tight end football guru at the University of Oregon for a month and a half. The second half of the summer would involve attending the UNC football camp and then conditioning until school started. "I know," I said with resignation.

Marcus looked at me, and I could see the care in his eyes. "I want you to promise me that since I am unavailable, that you will not hesitate to find a lover."

"Yes, sir," I said. "If I have to." My tone told him that I didn't want to comply but knew that it was pointless to argue.

"You have to," Marcus said firmly.

"Do I get to make a demand now, Master?" I asked, slipping back into our sexual personas.

Marcus suddenly got very serious. "Loch, I am only the Master when we are fucking around."

"I agree, Marcus. I would like to keep them separate."

"Good," he said, smacking me on the thigh. "And yes, you

can make a demand now."

"I want to live with you next year." There! It had been on my mind for two years, and I finally came out and said it. Instant relief flooded through my body.

"Loch, I would love that also, but you know what it is like when we are together."

"Yes, but I am willing to . . . curtail my activities to make this work."

Marcus narrowed his eyes and lowered his head, as if in disbelief.

"I will! We have always been good at setting boundaries and limits and then sticking with them."

"We have," he agreed.

"We can limit it to one fuck a night if you want to, and I will stay away from you on the night and mornings before game days."

"That's just it. I don't want to limit it to one fuck a night." Marcus' deep voice boomed. "We just can't help ourselves."

"If I have the chance to get fucked by you at least once a day, I will control myself," I promised him.

"It means that much to you?"

"Yes."

"It would save me a lot of time going from your dorm to mine."

"Yes, it would," I said, excitement coloring my voice as I realized that he was considering it.

"And we do really well studying together."

"Especially when we are in our special position," I said huskily.

He ignored my sexual salvo. "I will consider it."

"Thanks, Marcus!" I gushed as I turned on my side and put my head in the middle of his sweaty chest.

He hugged me to him with two muscled arms and said firmly, "I said that I will consider it, Loch."

"I know. But you have always said that you are the one who gives me what I need."

"Yeah, so?" he asked and then understanding crossed his face, his eyes twinkling with delight as I looked up at them. "Oh, so living together is what you need?"

"Yes," I said, laughing. "I want to immerse myself in the Marcus Battle experience . . . totally."

"You are the most amazing man I have ever met," he whispered.

"And you are mine," I whispered back.

"And I am yours," he said with a sigh.

CHAPTER TWO

Marcus and I were as committed to each other as ever, but I missed him terribly when I was home with my family outside of Charleston. I liked my family, but they couldn't hold my interest like Marcus Battle could. I was only home for two days before I called Mr. Lewellyn and got my old summer job back. He asked me to report directly to his office on Monday, and I assured him that I would.

Dad was pleased that I was going to work with Mr. Lewellyn again, because IBM paid so well that it would really help with the bills. Whenever my father talked of money, I immediately felt guilty that I had not joined The Service. That made me want him to never have to worry about money again. He had bought me a used car, saying that he had saved so much money since I received that scholarship from IBM that he could afford it.

In our world, marked men had the opportunity to attend a local Service Academy to learn the sexual arts of pleasuring NOMARs and could then enter into The Service. This was a program that contracted between marked men and wealthy NOMARs who wanted to have a sexual Servant. They paid handsomely for the use of the Servant, to the tune of a million dollars a year, and each contract could be extended if both parties agreed, for another year.

Sometimes, I wondered what our lives would have been like if I had gone to the SA and into The Service. I didn't regret not going, because I had always wanted to attend regular high school, and my dream was always to go to Chapel Hill. And besides, I would have never met Marcus.

How could any Master compare to him? They couldn't. But had I screwed myself out of the money? I could still enter into a contract after I graduated, if I desired, but the world made it very clear that nobody wanted an old Servant.

I knew my father would never say it, but I think he was disappointed about the chance at the money. Not only had I deferred my Service, but I had enrolled in college and cost him even more money. At least I was there on an academic scholarship and worked every summer.

I had a free weekend before I started work, so on Friday night I drove into the city and went to a new Turkish restaurant that I had read about in the paper. I got a lot of stares from the NOMAR patrons, as I always did when I was out in public, but since this restaurant was slightly classy, I felt secure. The food was amazing, and when my entrée came out, the waiter was followed by a young kid who started to dance.

He had a dark complexion and handsome features. He was dressed in a belly dancer costume and played the castanets loudly to piped-in music. The dancer was barefoot and not marked. I couldn't help but smile at him and applaud when the music was finished.

I left a nice tip when I paid for my meal and had every intention of going home when I left the restaurant. However, as I passed through the outdoor seating area to exit, I was immediately attracted to one of the patrons who was also eating alone.

He was probably in his early forties, with blond hair that was cut short. A square jaw with a blond beard framed a very handsome face. But to be honest, what stopped me in my tracks were the giant biceps that were stretching the arms of his red polo shirt to their limits. His left arm had a circular barb wire tattoo around the bicep and the other was tatted all over with tribal tats.

Feeling extra confident after the nice meal and the show, I

threw caution to the wind and sat down at his table. He was just finishing his meal and had a mouthful of curry when he looked up from his plate. His eyes registered surprise right before they locked in on my mark and realization hit him.

Waiting a few seconds as he finished chewing and swallowing, I finally introduced myself, "Hi, I'm Loch."

He held out his hand and said, "Kelly."

We shook, and his large rough hand ignited the fire in my crotch immediately. "I know this is extremely slutty of me to ask, but do you have plans tonight?"

"There's nothing wrong with being a little slutty," he said with a wink. "I was just going over to my friend's place to watch some TV."

"Call him and cancel," I commanded as I leaned back on the metal chair and smiled.

"Calling now," Kelly said as he grabbed his cell phone off of the table.

I laughed at his overt eagerness, which was only reflecting mine. I listened as he cancelled with his friend, Dave. Something had just come up and it required him to be home. Watching him, I couldn't help but think of how lucky I was to be that *something*. I was so damn picky now, thanks to Marcus setting the bar so high, that it usually took me weeks to find someone.

Kelly ended the call and looked up to see if I approved or not.

"Very good, Kelly."

He was already letting me control him like a puppet, and I had only known him for a minute or so. Kelly wasn't going to be someone that I could put up with long, but he would be good for a night at the very least. I started the questioning to decide how best to protect myself. "You live near here?"

"Yes."

"Alone?"

"No, with my brother."

"And he will be at home?"

"No, but he works the night shift, so we will be alone."

I smiled at him to let him know I was pleased. Grabbing my cell phone from my pocket, I sent a quick text to my father to let him know that I was going to spend the night at a friend's house.

"What's the address?" I demanded.

Kelly told me, and I added the address onto the end of the text to my dad. Just in case something happened, he would know where to start looking. My new friend watched me with great interest. I sent the message and said, "Let's go."

"I can drive," Kelly offered.

"I will follow you in my car," I said dismissively.

He threw down some money on the table and stood up. Kelly wasn't even going to finish his meal or wait for the check to arrive. He was a man of action, and I did appreciate that.

"So, what do you do, Kelly?" I asked as we walked to the cars.

"I own a gym," he answered, and involuntarily flexed his big biceps for me. "I know it is stereotypical of a meathead, but I've been able to franchise the business and have done quite well for myself."

"Sounds awesome to me. It's why you've kept in such good shape at your age, so I'm all for that."

"Speaking of age, how old are you, Loch?" he cautiously asked.

"Twenty."

"Holy fuck!" Kelly said excitedly.

"Your lucky day?" I asked with a chuckle.

"My lucky year," he gushed as I unlocked my car and then followed him to his house. Kelly drove a low-numbered Mercedes Benz, and his house was a modest ranch on the east side of town, I saw as we arrived.

We both parked in the driveway, and Kelly waited at his car for me. "This is it," he said with a flourish of his arm.

"It's nice, Kelly."

"I'm sure it is not nearly as nice as the mansions that you are used to."

"I haven't entered The Service yet, Kelly."

He looked surprised. "No? You must have been at one of those schools then. What do they call them? Service Academies?"

"That's what they call them, but I haven't been there either," I said as he unlocked the door.

He looked at me with a blank stare and I decided to put him out of his misery. "I decided to continue in my high school instead of going to the SA. Then I went to college at the University of North Carolina. That's where I am now. Going to be a junior."

He ushered me into the living room which was a huge man-cave. "So you've never had a Master?"

"Not in the traditional sense," I answered, thinking of my true Master, Marcus Battle.

"You want something to drink?"

I indicated the bottle of water that I had brought from my car and remembered getting drugged my freshmen year when I accepted a drink from a NOMAR at a party. I had learned to protect myself by always drinking my own stuff after that.

Kelly went to the kitchen and grabbed a beer while I had a seat between the pieces of workout equipment scattered around the room. His house smelled like musky men, sweat, and cum—a heady combination that made me a little light-headed.

"You want to pretend to be my Master tonight, Kelly?" I asked provocatively.

He swallowed hard and I loved watching his over-sized Adam's apple bob up and down on his thick throat. "Is that why you picked me?" he asked in a quiet tone.

"Is what why I picked you?"

"I'm so much older than you. Are you looking for a Master?" he asked innocently.

I laughed out loud and then quickly stopped when I saw that he wasn't joking. "No, Kelly, I asked you to fuck with me because you are my type—thick, hot, handsome, with a rocking body."

"Oh, I thought . . ."

"I asked if you wanted to try to be my Master, because I thought it might be a fantasy for you that you might be interested in."

The fog suddenly cleared. "Oh! Fuck yeah, it's always been my fantasy."

"So, you want to go for it?"

"Sure," Kelly answered, as he licked his lips in anticipation.

"Awesome," I commented as I stood up and moved in front of him. He followed my every move. Pulling off my shirt, I stepped out of my sandals and pushed my shorts to the ground. Stepping out of my shorts and just wearing my boxer-briefs, I assumed The Service Squat in front of him and heard his gasp as I did it.

The Service Squat was the position that all Servants were required to take when they met their Master for the first time. They also had to assume it whenever the situation did not provide any instructions to them about what to do. It was a general fallback position of subservience, and it hurt like hell.

I could tell that I was doing the squat correctly, because my thighs and back began to hurt immediately. In a full body squat, I was perched on the balls of my feet, my thighs were spread wide open, my forearms rested on each spread thigh, and my head was bowed. Marked men practiced this position at the SA constantly and could do it from sheer muscle memory, but I could not.

"I am yours to command, Master," I said, my head still bowed, my legs so shaky that I had to concentrate hard to keep from falling over. He obviously was not going to be a good dominant, because he had already let me undress and squat without telling me to do so.

"Holy shit," Kelly said under his breath.

Since there was no command, I squatted my ground.

"Uh, uh, go to my bedroom, Servant," he finally ordered.

"I don't know where your bedroom is located, Master," I said in a flat monotone voice.

"Shit! Follow me," he said, flustered as he stood and headed out of the living room.

I followed him down a wide hallway to a large bedroom that smelled like old sheets and cum. Even with my head bowed, I could see it was messy. There were even wads of Kleenex on the floor that I was sure were cum rags.

Kelly had begun to pick up the dirty clothes, so I assumed The Service Squat again and waited. He nervously apologized for the mess as he swept it under the bed or threw it into a hamper.

"Would Master like me to change the sheets for him?"

I lifted my head to see that Kelly looked at the bed for a second and then back to me. "Yes, Servant. Let me get you some clean ones." He left the room and came back with folded sheets that looked practically brand new.

I stood up and began to strip the bed. Kelly helped me and I couldn't help but notice the significant bulge in the front of his khaki shorts now. We soon had the bed made with clean sheets and the old ones in the hamper.

Kelly either seemed confused or nervous about what to do next, so I helped him out. "Would Master like me to undress him now?"

"Yes, please."

I walked to his side of the bed where he was standing and stood in front of him. He was only slightly shorter than me, probably six-two. I grabbed the hem of his red Polo shirt and lifted it over his head. Kelly lifted his big arms for me, and I had to really pull to get his bulging biceps out of those sleeves.

What I was left with was a great view of his chest and arms. He was shaven clean with no hair anywhere, including under his arms. His tattoos extended down his collarbone, but did not mar his great chest, pecs, or abs. He was thick, with just a slight beer belly behind his outie belly button.

Running my palms up his arms, I squeezed his biceps and felt him harden the muscles under my hands as I did. I smiled at him, and he returned it as I explored his chest with my hands, tweaking his nipples on the way.

Kelly moaned in pleasure, and I was soon removing his shorts and boxers. Kneeling in front of him, I was delighted to see that he had a big fat cock that jutted out of a completely shaven and smooth crotch. Wrapping one hand around his dick at the base, I put my other hand on his chest and pushed him down onto the bed.

He sat on the edge of the bed as I ran my hands down his big walnut-cracking thighs and down to his tennis shoes. Lifting one foot into my lap, I untied the strings and pulled his shoe off. His short sock was next, and I was impressed that his foot did not smell of anything but clean.

Rubbing his foot, I massaged it while Kelly looked at me in amazement. When I was finished, I did the same things to his other foot until he seemed to be totally relaxed.

Standing up, I slowly pushed my boxer-briefs down while twisting my body at the same time. This gave Kelly a slow look at my ass as it rotated in front of him—first covered, and then naked.

Kelly's fat cock responded to the sight of my ass as every NOMAR's did — by getting hard as a plank on a pirate ship.

Stepping out of my underwear, I knelt back in front of him, sat on my heels, and waited for his command. I knew what he wanted me to do, I knew how to give him greater pleasure than he could even ask for, but he wanted to be the Master, so I waited.

"Suck me," he said breathily.

I leaned forward and guided his hot cock into my mouth. My lips stretched to their limits to accommodate him, and all I could think about was how my asshole was going to have to do the same thing.

Kelly moaned above me as I used all my skills on him. He tasted clean, and I assumed that he had just showered before dinner since his feet and crotch smelled so nice. I pulled on his balls as I sucked and licked his fat member. He played in my blond hair with his hands as I serviced him.

I could feel that he was already on the verge of climaxing, so I put my thumb on the bottom vein right above his nut sack and pressed in, stopping his climax from coming so soon.

"On the bed," he ordered me. "I need to fuck that sweet ass of yours."

Okay, Kelly! Now, you're getting the hang of it.

I crawled onto the clean sheets. I didn't want to give him the chance to choose the position, because I knew since the second that I saw him that I wanted to be on my back underneath him. I wanted to swing from those big biceps as they held him up, so I lay down in the middle of the bed on my back.

"You need lube, Loch?" he asked, slipping out of Master mode.

"Yes, Master."

He startled at my use of the term and then grinned broadly as he grabbed a bottle of lube off the nightstand. Crawling back onto the bed, he looked unsure of what to do next.

Pulling my legs back onto my chest, I spread them wide and held them to me. "Can Master lube my tight hole for me?"

He looked at my puckered hole and then back to my face quickly. I don't think he'd ever considered doing this before, but to his credit, he jumped right in. Squirting lube on his fingers, he scooted closer to me and then rubbed the cool liquid right onto my rosebud.

Kelly didn't need to be told what to do next. He watched in fascination as my hole responded to his touch and then opened for him as he pressed a long thick finger onto it. His finger found its way completely inside of me and I groaned my pleasure to him. Kelly looked up briefly to see my face, then looked down again, beginning to fuck me with that finger.

"Another one, Master." I moaned.

Kelly added another finger inside me and then another. He seemed to really be enjoying himself and took his time pleasuring me until my cock was hard as the pirate's cutlass.

"I need your big cock inside me now, Master." I whined, my voice dripping with lusty promise.

"That's what I need, too," Kelly mumbled as he withdrew his fingers and knelt in the saddle between my legs.

He couldn't take his eyes off his cock as it slowly disappeared inside of me. "Fuck me!" he said a little too loudly as my asshole ate every inch of his girthy lap hog.

I used my ass muscles to squeeze his big dick as Kelly held us in place. He pushed me farther onto my upper back, lifting my ass off of the mattress, getting a better fit. Letting go of my legs, I placed them onto his broad shoulders and encouraged him to lean over me as he fucked.

Kelly was everything that I had hoped he would be when I first saw him—a good guy and a good fuck. He would serve his purpose, which was to keep me thinking clearly. With the itch in my ass scratched, I could focus on Marcus Battle and our eventual reunion at the end of July. When I fucked around with someone other than my boyfriend, it always made me miss him even more. No one compared with Marcus, and no one could take his place even for an hour.

Kelly fucked me hard and fast. He had pretty good stamina and didn't come right away once he was inside of me like most NOMARs. I held onto his tatted and straining biceps as he rocked his hips back and forth repeatedly until he lost his mind and flooded my ass with a big load of hot cum.

His handsome face was right above mine, and I watched as the most satisfied look came over his visage. Letting go of one big bicep, I moved my hand to his blond-bearded jaw line. Kelly looked like he was a Viking warrior who had just entered the gates of Valhalla.

Pulling my legs off of his shoulders, I wrapped them around his waist and onto his butt. I pulled him to me, fucking myself on his pole even more as he softened inside of me.

Kelly came back to himself and looked down at me. "God damn, that was fantastic!" He leaned to the side and rolled onto the bed beside me.

"You are not bad at that at all," I said with a chuckle. "Want to go again?"

"I wish! Your ass is so tight and hot, but I'm a one-and-done," he said, yawning.

Fuck! I had not planned on that.

Kelly added, "If you spend the night with me, I can go again in the morning." He ran a hand over my hip and ass as he said it.

Why not? At least the sheets are clean.

CHAPTER THREE

Kelly was true to his word. He had a raging boner in the morning that I wasted no time in sucking to its absolute hardest state. Kelly moaned and groaned as I sucked on his big joint, eventually whining that he wanted to fuck me again.

"Doggy style this time, Kelly?" I asked, seeing that he wasn't going to direct me.

"Fuck yes." He groaned as he popped up off the mattress.

I lubed myself after I got onto all fours in the middle of the bed. There was a mirror on the closet door in which I would be able to watch the tribal tatted behemoth tear me up.

Kelly crawled into the saddle, fed his fat dick into my tight hole, and began to let me have it. The only sounds I could hear were of our labored breathing, the smacking sound of his ball sack against my ass, and the slapping of our bodies together. That was why I didn't hear the man when he appeared.

"What the fuck are you doing?" the man in the doorway asked with a startled tone.

My head snapped up from between my shoulders, and I saw a tall, dark stranger filling up the doorway. He was wearing the uniform of a cop.

"Reggie!" Kelly said excitedly as he stopped fucking in mid-thrust. "This is Loch."

"Nice to meet you, Reggie," I said, just to break the awkwardness of the situation. Kelly had resumed nailing my ass from behind, so it was all I could do to keep myself up on all fours while looking at Reggie.

"Reggie is my brother and a cop, obviously," Kelly said,

accentuating each word with a thrust of his hips.

"Where the hell did you get a marked guy from, Kell?" Reggie asked his brother in disbelief.

"The question you should be asking is *Hey, Loch, how can I get in on this?*" I told him.

"Really?" Reggie asked, letting go of the door frame.

"Sure. You're practically in the middle of it already," I said, panting as Kelly reached his climax and roared as he filled me up with his hot spunk.

"You gotta try this hot hole, bro," Kelly said in choppy breaths.

Reggie started to strip his uniform off as Kelly gasped for breath against my back. He held his cock buried to the balls inside me until he went soft. Pulling out, he headed to the bathroom while I watched his brother undress.

Reggie had kept fit, even though he was older than Kelly, but had not overdone it. His chiseled chest was covered lightly with dark fur. He had the body of a working man and not a body builder, like his brother's.

Flipping onto my back, I could smell the cop's musk now. After a night of work in the summer heat wearing polyester, he was bound to smell.

"You want me to take a shower?" he asked me.

"We're not spending the night together, Reggie. I just want to suck on your big cock and have you fuck me silly."

He stared at me as he pulled his socks off and said, "I've never met a marked guy who was so cocky."

"He was the same way with me when he picked me up last night," Kelly said. Now, it was his turn to stand in the doorway.

"You better be cocky also," I said with a snort.

Reggie crawled onto the bed, and I saw he had a thick cock that was already semi-hard swinging between his legs. He knelt on the bed beside my head, reached down and put a big hand on my opposite side cheek, wrapping his fingers around the back of my head.

The dark cop pulled my head up and towards him as I opened my mouth to receive his nightstick. Sucking it into my mouth, I gave him a great blow, making sure that his big joint was sloppy wet with my spit before pulling off it. I knew he was ready because he was so hard and leaking a generous amount of delicious man-honey.

"You've done this before," I said to him, eyeing him suspiciously.

"You're not the first marked man who has offered me something," he said, his voice husky with lust. "Of course, I'm not about to arrest you."

"So, you've taken them up on it?" I asked with curiosity.

"Of course. I'm only a man," he said, beginning to laugh.

"Show me." I growled as I lifted my legs onto my chest.

He stared at my asshole and then back at my face. "All right then. You have the right to remain silent . . ."

I smiled and commented, "I don't think I will be very silent when that big monster is inside me."

The hot cop knelt between my legs, placed his cock on my puckered hole, and said, "Anything you say or do can and will be held against you in the court of law."

"I don't know about in court, but you better do more than hold it against me in this bed!"

"How's this?" Reggie asked as he pushed his hips forward and drove his big dick past my anal ring and into me.

"Oh, fuck." I moaned with my back arched and my head back.

"You have the right to speak to an attorney," the cop said, as he plumbed the depths of my ass with his big cock.

"I'm only going to need the attorney if you stop fucking me . . ."

His face stayed serious as he began to attempt to saw me in

half. His voice was completely steady and firm as he continued, "You have the right to speak to an attorney. If you cannot afford an attorney, one will be appointed for you."

"Oh, I'm getting the point." I groaned as Reggie's speed and intensity increased. He fucked me harder and faster with each stroke.

The big policeman's breathing became more erratic and deeper as he exploded with his climax. Holding my legs up and apart, he moaned the words, "Do you . . . understand . . . these rights . . . as they . . . have been . . . read to you?" Reggie busted his nut and filled my sore hole up with his hot cream.

"I understand my rights and I surrender, Officer. I will not resist arrest," I told him as I whacked my hard cock and blew a load of steaming spunk onto my stomach.

Reggie kept his big dick stretching my asshole out even as I jacked off, so he was able to feel my ass muscles clamp down on him when I came. He must have loved the feel of it, because he let go of my legs, bent over me, and fucked me again.

The cop, unlike his brother, did not have a problem coming more than once in a row. "I do like a nice tight hole," he finally said as he returned to himself after his second nut splash.

"I do like a good interrogation," I said with a wink.

Reggie rolled off of me and said to his brother, "You can bring this one home any time you want, Kell."

"I wish." Kelly sighed.

"You boys were a lot of fun," I said as I rolled off of the bed and headed to the bathroom to get cleaned up.

"You made our year, Loch," Kelly replied.

"I'll get your digits when I come out and maybe we can do it again."

"Soon, I hope," Reggie said luridly.

"You NOMARs," I said, shaking my head. "You just got to fuck me twice each, but you are still looking forward to the next time."

"Thank God for us." Kelly smirked.

"Thank God," I agreed.

When I was back in my car and headed home, I received a text from Marcus.

You get lucky last night?

How the fuck did he know that? *Yes, how did you know?*

You are reluctant to text or call me afterwards

I don't want you to be mad at me

Why would I be mad? I have commanded you to do this

I know, but I don't want you to ever think that there is anyone else but you

I know, you are mine

I am yours

And I am yours

You are mine

Now that we have that straight . . . were you safe?

Yes, sir

Good. Call me tonight.

With pleasure.

Remember to work out today

Of course. I must keep up with my Master

Yes, you must. LOL

Marcus had the power to make me feel better in an instant, and I couldn't believe how much I missed him.

CHAPTER FOUR

Saturday night, I decided to stay in with my family, and we watched a movie together. I spent most of Sunday watching golf, working out, and napping. Monday I started my summer job at IBM and was a little excited to either see the guys that I had worked on the line with last summer or to find out what job I would be doing this time around. And in all honesty, the thought of Mr. Lewellyn tying me up and fucking me hard also made me more than a little excited.

Walking into the boss' office that Monday morning, I said, "Hi, Mr. Lewellyn." Our relationship was still very formal, even though it was intimate.

"Loch!" he said with excitement. "How was your year at school?" He stood behind his desk and extended his hand.

I took his hand, shook it, and sat down in the leather chair he indicated. "It was good. How was your year?"

"Also good, although my Wednesday nights were never the same," he said with a smirk.

"Marcus enjoyed the benefit of some of our Wednesday nights," I informed him.

"I'm glad I could be of service," he said, bowing his head. "Shall we continue our arrangement?"

"Sure."

"And in which department would you like to work this summer?"

I had already considered that Mr. Lewellyn might ask this question, so I was ready with an answer.

"You will not be having the assembly line of college kids

like last year?"

"No. That adventure did not prove fruitful."

"Well, then I was thinking about Human Resources."

"Really?" he asked, somewhat surprised.

"I've been taking a lot of psych classes, and I do enjoy reading people," I explained to my older lover.

Mr. Lewellyn steepled his fingers in front of him and said, "That is a serious department, Loch."

"I can be serious."

"Yes, I've seen you when you were serious. Of course, you were usually restrained and gagged at the time." His voice dropped several octaves on the second sentence.

"I can be," I said, getting a little frustrated that I was trying to have a serious conversation with my boss when he was obviously horny as hell and was not being serious with me.

"We will give you a shot and see how it goes," Mr. Lewellyn decided instantly.

"Thank you."

"What?" The look on his face was the one he usually wore on Wednesdays when I had disobeyed some command.

"Thank you, sir," I quickly re-stated.

"You're welcome, Loch. You will report to Mr. Upton on the fourth floor."

"Can I do that now?"

"By all means. I will see you on Wednesday, if not before." Mr. Lewellyn stood and extended his hand.

I stood and shook his hand, both of us being very professional. When I left the office, I went down to the fourth floor and found the department of Human Resources. There was a receptionist who asked me why I was there.

I told him, "I am supposed to see a Mr. Upton."

I saw the look of surprise on the receptionist's face. "The Director?"

Nodding, I watched as he shamelessly stared at my mark,

and then there was a dawning comprehension that flooded his face.

"Have a seat."

The receptionist picked up a phone, turned sideways in his swivel chair, and lowered his voice as he spoke to someone.

When he hung up, he turned to me and said, "It will be a minute." He pretended to work in the next minute, but couldn't keep his side eye from looking at me.

Another man appeared, young and thin. He came right over to me and shook my hand. "I am the Director's assistant. Can I help you?" He was a very handsome Black man with an inscrutable face that he kept neutral at all times. I admired his control.

"My name is Loch. I am one of the college kids that they hire for the summer, and I was assigned to this department and told to report to Mr. Upton."

"I see. Well, fortunately, the Director has a few minutes before his meeting, so I will take you back to see him."

"Thank you," I said as I followed him.

The assistant to the director led me all the way to the back of the department, past many offices and conference rooms. The corner office was our destination, and Mr. Upton was standing at the door. He was an obese bald man who did not know that he was bald. He kept a few straggly strands of hair extra-long so that he could sweep them over his bald dome. His beady eyes roved over my body as I walked towards him, and he didn't even try to hide his excitement.

"Come right in," he said to me as he ushered me into my office. His puffy hand grazed my ass as he indicated a chair in which I should sit.

Even though I disliked him instantly, I decided to let it go. He sat beside me instead of behind his desk, which I thought was very strange.

"I'm Director Upton."

"Loch."

"Loch," he repeated. Leering at me, he said, "So, you have been assigned to the human resources department, have you?"

"Yes."

"I did not receive notification of that, and it is highly unusual for a . . . college kid to get assigned here."

"It just happened this morning."

"I see. Well, you are going to really enjoy being under my command," he said while he stared at my mark and licked his full lips.

I definitely will not be under your command.

"If you submit to me, Loch, you will have a very easy and enjoyable summer."

"Submit?" *There will be no submitting.*

His hand suddenly clamped down on my thigh and squeezed the inside of it. "You will appreciate my skills in the bedroom, Loch."

"And if I refuse?" I immediately asked.

He smiled greasily and answered with, "Then you will be . . . let go."

"Ever heard of sexual harassment, Mr. Upton? It is something that you should be working to eliminate in the workplace instead of promoting," I challenged him.

He looked surprised. "You are going to claim sexual harassment on your first day? Who would believe such an accusation? And you are a college kid who no one will believe anyway."

"You must be new here," I said with a smirk. "How long have you been here?"

He was immediately taken back by my brashness. "Two months. How did you know that?"

The time for answering his questions was over. Now it was my turn to tell him how this was going to go. "What's your assistant's name?"

Upton turned nervously toward the door and said, "Robinson, why?"

I snapped my fingers above my head and with a raised voice asked, "Robinson, can you come in here, please?"

Robinson immediately appeared at the door.

I stood, leaned back so I was resting against the fat man's desk and crossed my arms. "Robinson, did you just listen to our conversation?"

"No, sir," Robinson answered, with his neutral face not betraying his lie.

Upton grinned so broadly that he looked like a cartoon character. I also smiled, which confused him.

"Robinson, do you know who I am?"

He hesitated, and the mask of neutrality slipped a little. "I know who you are rumored to be," he said carefully.

"And who is that?" the Director snapped.

"They say that he belongs to Mr. Lewellyn, sir." His face was now one of panic.

I grinned even more broadly as I watched the horror cross Upton's face. "Well, I do not belong to him, but I am under his protection. In fact, I just came from his office. Now, I will ask you again. Did you just overhear that conversation, Robinson?"

"Yes, sir," he immediately answered.

"Thank you, Robinson. You can go." When Robinson had left, I turned to Upton and asked, "Would you like to keep your job?"

"Yes, please."

"I will think about it. In the meantime, you will never touch me again or even speak to me without my permission. Do you understand?"

"Yes."

"You will tell Robinson to assign me to your best senior manager and tell him to treat me like any other intern. If word gets out that I am connected to Lewellyn, I will not be happy with you."

"I can't control rumors," he sputtered.

"Then you'd better hope that they do not arise," I threatened.

He shook his head while looking down.

"Well, I'm waiting," I said with obvious exasperation.

Upton looked up at me suddenly, and then he realized that I was serious. "Robinson," he called.

"Yes, sir," Robinson said from the doorway.

Upton turned to face him and said, "We can never speak of Loch's relationship to Mr. Lewellyn again."

"Yes, sir."

"Assign him to Drew Jarrett as an intern."

"Jarrett, sir?" When he saw the look on Upton's face, he immediately said, "Yes, sir."

"If Jarrett is not the best, I will be back," I threatened Upton.

"He's the best," Upton said nervously.

I didn't say anything else, but instead headed towards the door. Robinson turned to walk out in front of me and we headed down the hallway. Turning towards me, he said, "Jarrett really is the best. I'm sorry that I lied to you in there, but he would have fired me if I had told the truth."

"I figured as much. Upton's an ass."

"I like you already!" Robinson said with a big grin. "This is Drew's office," he said, stopping in front of a suite of rooms.

A secretary or assistant stood up, looking confused until he saw Robinson behind me.

Robinson said, "Daniel, this is Loch. He is going to be Mr. Jarrett's intern for the summer."

"What?" Daniel asked. His eyes had flicked to my mark and stayed there.

Robinson ignored his question. "Please let Mr. Jarrett know

that he is here."

"Of course," Daniel said, finally able to get himself under control. "Loch, please have a seat, and I will let him know."

I sat down, Robinson left, and Daniel disappeared into an office. He came back with a short stocky guy in a very expensive suit, obviously tailored to fit his unique body type. He was bald, with a full brown beard that started right at the top of his ears. His brown eyes alertly took in everything about me.

"I'm Drew Jarrett," he said, as he stepped in front of his assistant and held out a manly hand for me to shake. I took it and enjoyed how hard he squeezed my hand.

"Loch," I informed him.

"I hear that you are going to be working under me this summer?" he said without the slightest hint at the sexual innuendo that he was throwing my way.

Yes, Drew Jarrett, you will work nicely, and I definitely will be working under you this summer.

CHAPTER FIVE

Mr. Jarrett was nothing if not professional. He took me to his office and accepted me just like any NOMAR intern. He made absolutely no move to flirt with me nor said anything that was lurid or inappropriate. That in itself was refreshing and made me even more horny for him than I already was. He showed me the ropes in the morning and gave me my first assignment in the afternoon.

After lunch, I entered the elevator and hit the button for the second sub-basement. As soon as the doors opened, I saw a sign indicating the Maintenance Department, so I turned right and headed down a dingy hallway. Unlike the rest of the building, this floor was not decorated, with walls that were not even painted or finished in some places.

The Maintenance Department doors were open, apparently never closing. I walked through them and right into a big room dominated by a table where three guys were seated playing cards.

"Whoa!" one of them said, partially standing and dropping his cards when he saw me.

"Sorry, fellas," I said quickly.

"Well, well, well," the older one said, looking at my mark. "What is this?"

I noticed right away that all three of them were cute—handsome in that rugged hyper-manly way. "I'm Loch from HR. Mr. Jarrett sent me down to see Mr. Waylon."

"Mr. Waylon?" the middle aged one asked with a funny look at the older one.

"I'm Bill," the older one said. "This is Jake and the young-ster is my son, Rick." Bill was in his fifties, Jake in his forties, and Rick was somewhere around my age.

"Bill Waylon?" I asked.

"Yes."

"Mr. Jarrett says that I am to collect the incident report from you from last week's accident."

"I'm still working on it," he said sullenly.

I told him, "He says that I am not to leave your side until I have it."

"Is that right? Well, I guess you will have to have a seat and play a hand."

"Not while I'm on the clock. I can help you complete the form if you need me to," I told him, taking a seat on the empty side of the table.

"Should we switch to strip poker?" Jake asked, his voice husky with lust.

I answered quickly to regain the upper hand. I was deter-mined to come out successful in this first assignment for Mr. Jarrett. "Maybe after work one day, fellas, but not during."

All of their faces snapped up to mine, and I knew I had their complete attention now.

"Wow! You would really do that or are you just making empty promises to get that form?"

I was ready for that question also, so I let the hammer drop. "Not if I don't get that form . . ."

Rick and Jake both turned with hopeful expressions to the oldest maintenance man. "All right," Bill finally relented. Rick stood up, walked over to an old rickety file cabinet, and pulled out a piece of paper. He walked over to the table and handed it to me.

I looked at the accident report and saw that the checklists had been completed, but the lower section was blank. "You need help with the writing?" I asked the oldest maintenance man.

"Yeah, I'm not so good at that part," Bill said. His voice was tinged with embarrassment and wounded pride.

"I just happen to be excellent at that part, Bill." I pulled a pen out of my pants pocket and took the cap off of it. "Can you describe what happened? And I will write it out for you."

Bill started to tell the story, which involved being on a ladder while he was changing a light bulb. The ladder lost its footing and he had fallen. He had landed hard on the carpeted floor and been cut by the broken glass from the light bulb, as well.

I asked Mr. Waylon a few questions about it and then told the workers that they could finish their game while I finished the form. Writing down a concise narrative of the story Bill had told me, I finished in a flourish and waited for the three friends to finish their hand of cards before saying anything.

"Just sign here and I will get this form filed for you."

"You have just turned out to be a real help, Loch," Rick said. "There are not many people in this whole building that I can say that about."

"That's what I'm here for," I said with a smile as I stood.

Jake suddenly asked, "And what about that strip poker game, Loch?"

"Let me know when you boys want to be schooled," I said over my shoulder as I walked out the doors.

Mr. Jarrett couldn't believe it when I reported back with the accident form. "We've been asking for that form for a solid week," he said in amazement.

"All he needed was someone to go down there," I said humbly.

"I sent four people down there before you," Mr. Jarrett said drolly. He looked up at me and seemed to be studying me. "I think you may be a real asset to this department, Loch. Good work!"

I was more than happy that he was pleased with me. "Thanks, Mr. Jarrett."

"Tell Daniel to find you an empty office to get set up in. Tomorrow and the next day, we will be interviewing."

"Yes, sir."

I couldn't wait to get home and talk to Marcus. He was happy that my first day had gone so well, but he wanted to kill Mr. Upton, and he worried about me flirting with the maintenance guys. He told me to be extra careful in that big building of lusting NOMARs. Marcus was leaving for Oregon the next morning, so we spent the rest of the call talking about that.

I had hoped to see some of my old friends from the assembly line that we'd worked on during the last summer break, but had not so far. Interviewing the next two days was really boring. Mr. Jarrett had told me that he wanted me to sit in on several of them and then record my thoughts about each one.

I had to admit that I think I was a distraction to most of the guys as they tried to answer the interviewer's questions. They weren't sure why I was there, and they seemed to find me a total mystery as I wrote in a small notebook. One interviewee actually accused Jarrett of having me there to see what the candidates would do under a stressful situation.

Mr. Jarrett seemed very pleased with my notes and impressions. He told me that I seemed to be an excellent judge of character and a professional people reader. I basked in his praise, but he didn't seem to be falling under my spell like most NOMARs did. In that regard, he reminded me of Marcus Battle.

Wednesday after work, I went to the gym, worked out, and then waited for Mr. Lewellyn in the parking lot. I had moved my car into the empty space beside his dark blue BMW. I figured that we were going to go to our usual room at the Hyatt, but didn't want to chance it if his plans had changed.

I saw Mr. Lewellyn in my rear-view mirror as he exited the gym and walked towards the cars. He was fifty-five, but looked in better shape under his dark suit than even last year. He was bald, but had a striking white goatee. He approached the driver's side window. I studied his face, noticing that his very active eyes took in everything as his body carried him forward. His sense of confidence was very attractive to me.

"Hey, Loch," he said when I rolled my window down.

"Hey, sir. Are we going to the Hyatt?"

"No. I thought we would go to my home tonight."

I was shocked to hear this, because all of last year we had fucked and I had never been to his house. "Don't you have a Servant there, sir?"

"Not anymore. I let Brandon go in the Spring and have not called for another one yet."

"Okay," I agreed. "Lead the way."

My boss smiled and jumped in his sports car. I followed him to a very upscale housing development far outside the city. It was gated and had heavy security. His house was a behemoth and completely automated. The moment he stepped into it, the lights came on low, music started to play, and CNN appeared on multiple monitors throughout the house.

"Beautiful," I said in awe, looking around.

"You will probably have a house like this one day, Loch, after you complete your Service, of course," he told me while observing my interest in his home.

I nodded to Mr. Lewellyn, but I knew in my heart that I would never have a house like this. Having already come to the conclusion that I was going to give up my chance to enter into The Service in order to stay with Marcus, I had chosen my path. I would never be rich, at least not from The Service contract. But I had not told anyone about that decision, not even Marcus, so I was certainly not going to tell my boss.

Mr. Lewellyn's expression slowly changed to one of lust and need. "Kneel, Loch."

I fell to my knees on the hardwood floors immediately.

My boss reached in a cabinet and retrieved something that I couldn't see. He walked over to me and around me. He touched the piece of leather to my face and then let it rub my skin as he completed another loop. When he stopped in front of me, he snapped a leather collar around my neck and buckled it into place.

"On all fours," he commanded.

I fell forward onto my outstretched hands. It immediately crossed my mind that Mr. Lewellyn might be really pent up if he had been without a Servant for a couple of months. I was about to find out how true that impression was.

My boss snapped a chain onto my collar and then walked ahead of me. He had leashed me like a dog. Suddenly, I had to follow him or hurt my neck. Scrambling to keep up with him, I felt the pain in my knees from the floor. Thankfully, we soon moved onto carpet and then to a doorway with stairs leading down. They were carpeted also, fortunately.

I carefully negotiated the stairs on all fours. Mr. Lewellyn was patient with me as I figured it out and then he led me to a locked door. Producing the key from his pocket, he unlocked the door and the lights automatically lit.

This room was a dungeon. It was not the romantic playroom of some of the recent popular bondage romance books. This was a real working dungeon — grey slate walls and floor, wall sconces that were made to resemble flaming torches, and of course, the instruments of bondage. I let my gaze flick over the iron cross, stocks and pillory, a whipping bench, a mattress, and a rack.

I turned wide eyes on Mr. Lewellyn and said, "You told me that I would never be hurt."

"And you will not. I love to bind you, Loch. I am not a

sadist who has to inflict pain to get off." He swept the room with a hand and informed me, "These are all instruments to keep you bound."

I nodded, trusting him for the time being.

"Good. Now, strip."

"Yes, sir." I followed his command and stripped completely naked.

"Kneel." Once I was kneeling on the cold slate floor, he stood in front of me and asked, "What would you like to work on this summer, Loch? What would you like the focus of our work to be this year?"

This was not a question that I was prepared to answer because it had never occurred to me he would ask it. I had never thought of our sessions as trainings, until now.

"I didn't know this had to have a focus, sir."

"All training has a point, Loch. Last summer, your focus was to get to know me, trust me, learn about bondage and come to appreciate its merits. Didn't you accomplish that?"

"I did." I blushed as I remembered how much Marcus and I had enjoyed what I had learned from last summer.

"So, what shall it be this summer, then?" he challenged me again.

Thinking quickly, I soon realized that I had known what I needed all along. "Patience, sir. I need to learn patience."

"And why is that, Loch?"

"I would like to move in with my . . . boyfriend, and if he allows it, I will need to exercise patience, and I'm afraid that I'm pretty bad at it, sir." I had almost said that I wanted to move in with my Master. I had become aware that Marcus was my true Master and I thought of him as such, but I did not want Mr. Lewellyn to know that.

A true Master was someone of myth or legend in the marked community. Very few of us ever found our true Masters. True Masters were supposed to be the exact embodiment of what a marked man needed sexually — a true fit in every way. It was rare and impossible to find, but it was what all marked men strove for. And I was pretty sure that I had found mine.

"Very well. We shall make that our focus. Stand."

I stood as Mr. Lewellyn walked to a trunk, pulled out a blindfold and covered my eyes with it. Once I was blindfolded, he put the palm of his hand on the middle of my chest and backed me across the room.

"Step up," he commanded.

I stepped up and back onto a wooden board. Mr. Lewellyn secured my ankles and wrists.

"There. That is more like it."

I heard my boss unzipping his fly and then struggling to get his big dick out of it. Excited to get fucked, I licked my lips in anticipation. Suddenly there was a clicking sound, and then the platform I was strapped to begin to spin. I guessed that I was on the Wheel of Fortune.

Mr. Lewellyn let his cockhead touch my face and then my lips as it slowly went around the circle. I opened my mouth for the next pass, but he kept me spinning.

And suddenly he was gone.

CHAPTER SIX

Mr. Lewellyn did not return for quite some time, but then again, it was hard to keep track of time when I was blindfolded and strapped upside down on a wheel. I wondered if this was my first test of patience or whether he had been distracted by something more important. I marveled at the amount of patience it must have taken for him not to fuck with me, since he had been without a Servant for months now.

After what I deemed to have been a sufficient amount of time waiting for him, I began to whimper softly. I gave that a few minutes, and when I realized that I was getting no response from my boss, I moved on to begging and pleading. For all I knew, he could have been sitting right here in the room with me and I never would have known it.

Suddenly, I heard the door open and footsteps crossed the room towards me. Mr. Lewellyn had changed his footwear from dress shoes to something heavier, like boots.

I took the opportunity to beg directly to him, "Please, sir."

"Finding it hard to be patient, Loch?" I could hear the smirk in his voice.

"Yes, sir."

He stopped right in front of me, based on the closeness of his breath on my legs. "I have noticed that when most things have been taken from you, Loch, that you continue to try to manipulate the situation with your mouth."

I knew he was right. I was always trying to gain the upper hand, and it was usually with my mouth. "Yes, sir."

"Don't speak unless I ask you a question, Loch."

I closed my mouth, realizing for the first time that this summer experience with Mr. Lewellyn was truly going to be more than last summer's vanilla introduction to bondage.

Something hard came down on my belly and stung. "While you are waiting for me, you will remain hard. Do you understand, Loch?"

"Yes, sir." This was no problem for me—I just had to think of Marcus Battle and I was hard instantly.

"Good. Now, you may suck my cock, college boy," Mr. Lewellyn said lustfully. He spun the wheel until I stopped sideways at the perfect height to suck his big wiener.

Sucking Mr. L's fat sausage into my mouth, I savored the pre-cum that he was leaking and reveled in the fact that I could easily swallow all of him.

Thank you, Marcus!

I had never sucked a dick sideways before and was definitely at a disadvantage by not being able to use my hands, but I made the most of it. My boss was soon grunting above me as he drove his legs and hips forward—driving that big piece of meat between my lips over and over.

Mr. Lewellyn came in a tidal wave of cum that threatened to choke me, so I swallowed quickly and spit the rest back onto his cock. He held my head as he rubbed his cummy knob on my lips and said, "That was really good, Loch. Now, clean your Master up."

Using my tongue and lips, I suctioned the cooling cum from his big stick. My ass itched deep inside because it knew what was next and it wanted his big cock inside it as much as my mouth had.

"Would you like to be fucked now, Loch?"

"Yes, sir," I answered honestly.

Mr. Lewellyn didn't respond, but he did unshackle my wrists and then my legs. I had been on the Wheel so long and was still blindfolded, so I was a little unsteady on my feet. He held me to his strong frame as he moved me to a bench.

"Lie across it, Loch." His voice was very firm, and I wondered if I had upset him in some way.

Reaching out and touching the table, I felt that it was padded on two sides — the top and the side I was facing. It was a spanking bench, and my breath caught in my throat as I imagined Mr. Lewellyn wearing me out with a belt or cane.

"Now!" he commanded.

I lay forward over the top of the bench, bent at the waist. My boss quickly and efficiently snapped my wrists and ankles into restraints, stretching me over that bench. My ass was fully exposed, and I braced myself for the hit.

It never came. Instead Mr. Lewellyn left the dungeon again.

Shit! I mean, I know that I asked for us to work on patience, but can't that be after he gives me a hard, deep fucking?

I was left with an insistent itch in my ass and a very annoying need to be fucked. Lying across the bench, I thought about how much I would enjoy being strapped to this bench with Marcus. That thought sustained me as I waited. My cock was painfully pressed between my stomach and the bench.

Mr. Lewellyn came back a few minutes later, and I smelled food. My stomach growled instantly as I heard him pull a chair up to my head. "Open your mouth, Loch."

I did, and he pushed a spoonful of what tasted like chicken and rice into my mouth. It was good and I swallowed it quickly, not realizing until then how hungry I had been. Mr. Lewellyn continued to feed me and let me sip from a water bottle until he was finished.

"You want me to fuck that sweet ass now, Loch?"

"Yes, sir." I practically pleaded with my tone of voice.

"Wait right here for me," he said with a smirking tone as he left again. I couldn't see the look on his face when he was leaving, but I could hear it in his voice.

"Yes, sir."

My boss turned around and then walked to the cabinet,

based on the footsteps and scraping drawer sound I heard. "That did not require a response from you, Loch." He soon appeared back at my head. "Let's see if this helps with that," he said, as he put a piece of rubber tubing between my teeth and held it in place with a strap on my head.

It did help, but I hated it, of course. I needed to surrender, and I just couldn't. Not to Mr. Lewellyn. To Marcus, of course, I could surrender and completely give myself to him. I had complete confidence that I belonged to him and that gave me the freedom to surrender. Even though I liked him a lot, there was no way I could let that happen with my boss.

With Mr. Lewellyn, I naturally tried to fight for control. He was right to restrain me in every way possible, because I could not stop from trying to manipulate every situation and person that I met. Mr. Lewellyn knew this, of course and was taking steps to circumvent it.

My summer boss came back to the dungeon while I was still lost in my thoughts. He stayed behind me as I was bent over that whipping bench. I heard the unmistakable sound of lube being applied and I smiled around my gag, anticipating having my itch scratched real soon.

Mr. Lewellyn caressed my ass and even spanked it a few times, but his heart was not in it. He opened my ass cheeks and rubbed his thumb across my puckered hole, sending red shockwaves running up my spine. I was so ready to be fucked that I was practically drooling around the gag in my mouth.

Mr. L placed something hard and cold on my rosebud and slowly pushed it through my anal ring. I could tell right away that it wasn't his cock — it was too hard, too cold, and not susceptible to my ass muscles.

He was going to fuck me with a dildo when we both needed his cock inside me so desperately, or so I thought. I wanted nothing more than to scream at him to fuck me, but the gag prevented me from doing that.

I soon had other things on my mind. Mr. Lewellyn knew how to work over someone with a sex toy, that was for sure. He sawed that thing back and forth inside of me, constantly changing the angle. It gave me a great amount of pleasure having my ass sliding up and down that fake dick, but it was not scratching that itch deep down inside of me.

"You like that, Loch?" he asked in a husky voice.

I moaned my response the best I could.

"You want me to fuck you with my big hard cock now, Loch?"

"Yes." I moaned. It sounded nothing like the word.

"I thought you might," Mr. Lewellyn said with a chuckle. "But, I don't think you are ready just yet." He pushed a butt plug into me, stretching my hole temporarily before it settled into place, doing nothing but annoying me.

"Please," I whined, but it came out like, "pppppwwwweee." It was to no avail, because I could hear him walking out the door even before I finished whining.

I waited, this time trying to control my vocalizations. I refused to whine or beg, just in case Mr. Lewellyn was listening. Controlling my heartbeat, I forced myself to relax. Moments later, the door opened and he stepped inside the dungeon. He came up behind me and pulled the butt plug out of me.

"You've been very patient, Loch, so it is time for your reward now."

Thank God!

Mr. Lewellyn parted my ass cheeks and placed his dark purple dart-shaped cock head onto my rosebud. I couldn't see it, but I had spent enough time with it that I knew it like my own.

Not showing much patience himself, he manager soon thrust his hips forward and filled my anal channel with his long piece of man-meat. I pushed my ass back to meet him, ensuring that every single sixteenth of an inch of his hot cock was inside of me.

"Oh, fuck! Where have you been all year, Loch?" he moaned from behind me.

I didn't try to respond, but tears ran down my face as my itch was finally getting scratched.

My boss proceeded to rail me out with his big cock. He fucked me hard and fast, urgent for his release. I was not the only one who needed a lesson in patience. When he came, he collapsed onto my back and filled my ass with hot cum.

Mr. Lewellyn absentmindedly ran his fingertips over my sweaty back as he came back to himself. He started to talk to me, and I found the one-sided conversation to be slightly on the disturbing side, so I kept quiet and started to try to think a way out of the situation.

"So tight and so hot for me, Loch."

"I wish I could convince you to be my Servant. I would pay you handsomely."

"Your ass makes my cock feel like it is the first and only one to ever fuck you."

"I hope Marcus treats you like the treasure you are."

"I could make you happy, Loch."

"You make me happy."

I was starting to wonder how attached Mr. Lewellyn was getting to me as he said these things. It would be uncomfortable when we finished, not to mention for the rest of the summer, if I didn't address it as soon as I could.

Maybe it was just post-sex talk that he didn't really mean.

Mr. Lewellyn unbuckled the rubber gag from my head as he started to fuck me again. I didn't fail to notice that he had not removed his dick from my ass. I worked my lips back and forth to have them feel normal again just as he worked his member the same way in my ass. Running my dry tongue over my abused lips, I celebrated in the sensations that were dominating my nervous system — he was slamming my body against the bench, his cock prodding my prostate repeatedly, his big sweaty hands on my hips, manipulating them to his advantage, my cock being ground and pressed into the leather cushion, and my mind reeling with the possibilities of how I could use all of this with the only man I wanted to experience it with, Marcus Battle.

My boss kept his lower body pressed against mine as he sawed my ass back and forth on his shaft, which caused my hard cock to rub on the leather bench pad until my release built to an unbearable level. He erupted again just as I reached my own climax, pumping thick white goo all over the spanking bench and my sweaty skin.

"Welcome home, Loch," Mr. Lewellyn said as he lay exhausted across me.

CHAPTER SEVEN

A nd so the summer progressed. Marcus and I texted and called each other daily. I was proud of him for working so hard on improving his football skills and he was proud of me for continuing to work out even when he was not with me to force me into it. I was jealous as hell of the workers at the Service Station where he was going to blow a load and release some steam. And he, of course, did not want to hear anything about my sexual exploits, except whether I was being safe and regularly getting fucked to keep my head straight.

Mr. Lewellyn made sure that I got my twice weekly fucking and that I learned my lessons on patience. On one of our weekends away together, he strapped me to a bed spread-eagled and hung a countdown clock from the ceiling above the bed. I learned quickly that every time I whined, grunted, moaned or moved, the countdown clock would reset itself.

Mr. Lewellyn refused to come back into the room in which I was bound until the countdown clock reached zero each time. Upon a successful wait, I would be rewarded with a hot load of spunk down my throat or a hard fucking, and then the clock would be restarted. It didn't escape my attention that each reset involved adding additional minutes to the clock. By the end of that first weekend, I could go almost an hour without a sound or movement.

Our next weekend away, we were joined by Mr. Lewellyn's brother, Richard, and his lover, Bill. I had met them last summer and heard the story of how the two had fallen in love with each other. Richard was a NOMAR who enjoyed being fucked, and his favorite cock to ride was his childhood friend's. I had witnessed it last summer as Mr. Lewellyn fucked me hard on one side of the bed while his brother was getting drilled by Bill on the other.

Bill, Richard and Mr. Lewellyn kept my mouth and hole very busy that weekend. I was constantly being filled with cum, and fortunately for me with Richard there, I got to fuck him often to relieve the pressure in my own nuts. Richard and I had a common bond and I enjoyed talking to him about the pleasures of getting fucked and the lessons that his brother was teaching me.

By the end of my summer break in Charleston, I could go without moving for up to two hours, and in our last session, Mr. Lewellyn waited until the end of the whole weekend before he fucked me. He must have been pent up, because once he started, he fucked me four times in a row before unstrapping me, bathing me, and carrying me to his car. I had been dying to be fucked all weekend, and to have to wait almost two days for it was excruciating for me, but it was a lesson well-learned.

Mr. Lewellyn was driving us back to Charleston when he asked me, "So, Loch, I guess you will be heading back to school this week?"

"Yes, sir. I'm going up on Friday."

"Will I see you on Wednesday after the gym?"

"No, sir. I promised my family that I would go out to dinner with them to celebrate my brother's birthday."

"I will miss you, of course. Will you work for me next summer?" And by asking me that, I knew that he meant work at the factory as well as lie under him on a regular basis.

"Will I be receiving the IBM scholarship this year, Mr. Lewellyn?" I answered his question with one of my own.

"Of course," he said smoothly.

"Then, yes," I said with a lazy grin. I didn't mind working

at the factory nor fucking around with my boss.

"Your man is very, very lucky," Mr. Lewellyn said, looking out at the road, almost to himself.

"Yes, we both are," I agreed. "And we are also lucky to have a benefactor like you, boss." I turned and smiled at him.

He grabbed the inside of my thigh with a big hand and shifted his beady eyes to my face. "Yes, I have been very fortunate to have found you, Loch."

His touch made my crotch catch fire once more and I suddenly remembered something I had wanted to ask him. "Mr. Lewellyn, can I ask you something about what happened at the cabin?"

He looked stunned for a second and removed his hand from my thigh. "Of course . . ."

"How in the hell did you wait all weekend to fuck me?"

"Not very patiently," he said, laughing so hard he started coughing.

"No, seriously," I said to him.

He ended his coughing jag and said, "I practice something called edging."

"Edging?" I repeated, thinking back to figure out if I had ever heard the term before. I couldn't think of a time that I'd ever heard it.

"It's when you bring yourself to the edge of climax and then stop."

"Really?" I asked, wondering if it could really be that simple.

"It's supposed to be an even greater high than climaxing, but I have to tell you, Loch, that it doesn't even come close to being inside your sweet ass before, during, or after coming." He smiled at me and tousled my hair.

"How do you keep from automatically coming once you are on the edge?"

"Drop your pants and I will show you."

"What?"

"Drop your pants, Loch," he growled.

I lifted up, balancing between my feet and my back. Sliding my shorts and underwear to the floorboards, I grabbed my cock and looked over at my boss.

"Jack your cock, Loch."

I did as he commanded. It was easy enough to just remember the raging four fucks he had just given me. I was hard in no time.

"Now, right when you are on the edge, you press here." He leaned over and touched a spot behind my balls. "And here," he said as he pressed another spot on the base of my cock. "When you press them together while you are on the edge, you will experience a whole new sensation."

I kept pumping my cock until I was there and the urge for release was so strong that I could think of nothing else. I awkwardly pressed on the two spots Mr. Lewellyn had just shown me, looking at him to make sure that I was doing it correctly. My cock remained rock-hard, but the urge for release dissipated instantly. I couldn't help but be left with the sensation that I was missing something or that something bad had happened. It was not a rewarding sensation at all, but I could see how it would be helpful if I were delaying your gratification.

"Do you think Marcus will enjoy that?" Mr. Lewellyn asked.

I laughed out loud at his words. "I would never want Marcus to delay his climax, and I'm sure that he would never even consider it!"

"It might be the only way that he can . . . sustain himself for long periods of time," Mr. Lewellyn offered. My boss obviously did not know my boyfriend. Marcus could fuck for hours at a time, cumming multiple times without a break and never going soft. He was a machine—a wonderful, dream-come-true machine that loved to fuck.

"He has absolutely no problem with that," I told Mr. Lewellyn, continuing to laugh.

"Perhaps *you* can use it then," he offered.

"Marcus would not let me stop my climax, because he would have a tighter hole to fuck the next time," I explained. "But it is a good little trick to know. I'm sure that it will come in handy with other . . . less Godlike mortals than you and Marcus Battle."

My boss laughed easily. "You know, I'm going to miss you."

"I know. You'll have to ask for another Servant, because you won't be able to make it without one."

"I already have," he said with a wink. "I asked for someone just like you. They are still looking . . ."

I chuckled and looked out the window. Mr. Lewellyn grabbed my thigh again, causing me to turn and look at him.

"You know that after school is over next year, that I would gladly call for you and make you a millionaire."

"Thanks, boss. I will keep that in mind."

He looked a little surprised and asked, "I thought your plan was to enter into The Service when you graduate?"

"It is."

"Oh, but you're unsure whether you want me to call for you or not," he hypothesized.

"I've never really given it any thought, to be honest with you. I just feel like I have the perfect set-up, and I will be really sad when it goes away," I said with such honesty that he didn't seem to be able to refute it.

"You would be happy here . . . with me . . . and Richard and Bill," he finally said as we pulled into the parking lot of IBM.

"Yes, I would."

I hugged Mr. Lewellyn goodbye once my bag was placed into my car, and he hugged me back a little too long. Jumping in my car, I pulled out my cell phone and called Marcus.

"Hey, Loch," he greeted me warmly. "Are you back from the hotel with Mr. Lewellyn?"

"Yes. How's football camp going?"

"I'm glad that you are safe. Camp is wearing me out."

I paused, warring with myself about what I really wanted to ask him. Deciding to go for it, I say, "Camp is wearing you out, or the football orgy wore you out?"

The party on the middle weekend of football camp was legendary. The coaches hired a lot of willing employees from local Service Stations to come to the University and hold a party on Saturday night. The rumors surrounding this party ran rampant among the students once school started back in August.

"Believe me, those boys couldn't wear me out. There's only one person who can do that." His voice had turned from warm to husky with lust in a heartbeat.

"Oh, yeah?" I could listen to him say things like that all day long. I loved that he had it as bad for me as I did for him.

"Yeah. Coach Conway wears me the fuck out."

"Coach Conway?" I asked in dismay.

"I'm just kidding with you, Loch. You are the only one who can truly make me collapse from exhaustion."

"My big strong man didn't find a hole he liked last night?"

"I found some, but they were not what I'm used to . . ."

I giggled in response. I loved that he loved fucking me as much as I loved being fucked by him.

When he spoke again, his husky voice was back. "You coming up to see me this week?"

"Planning on it."

He timidly asked, "Do you have something special planned?"

Marcus might have been remembering last summer's camp, when he returned to the locker room to find me bound naked and spread-eagled in front of his locker. He had fucked me so hard and deep that day that we actually broke the binding apparatus I had borrowed from Mr. Lewellyn.

"I might," I answered evasively. I had been planning my surprise all summer with Mr. Lewellyn's help. It was elaborate, and I wasn't even sure that I was going to be able to pull it off.

"That will be my true party then." He growled. "I can't wait!"

"You better wait," I threatened.

"Friday can't come soon enough, that's all I'm saying." I could hear in his voice that he wasn't just saying the words, but that he felt them.

I smiled into my phone. "You have a day off from camp today?"

"Yeah. I'm going to go work out and then run some drills on the field with Coach Conway," Marcus told me.

"That doesn't sound like a day off to me," I scoffed.

"It's one for me though, since that is all that I'm doing. What are you doing?"

"I have to do laundry and start packing. You got us somewhere to crash until school starts?" I asked, prying into his plans.

"I got you," my big man said mysteriously.

"Yes, you do. Talk to you tomorrow, you big lug."

"See ya!"

CHAPTER EIGHT

My last week of summer vacation at home drug by ever so slowly. It was like waiting for Christmas Day to come, but in this case, I knew exactly what my presents were going to be—a super-hot Marcus Battle, his big thick cock, and plenty of his delicious man-cream inside of me.

I worked at IBM that last week just to stay busy and spent every night with my family, playing games and eating out at my favorite restaurants. Fortunately, I did not run into Mr. Lewellyn at all the last week, so there was very little awkwardness before I left. I packed all my stuff and loaded my car for the drive to Chapel Hill on Friday morning.

When I emerged from my room with a giant gift-wrapped present, I got several stares from my father and brothers. "It's a present for Marcus," I mumbled.

"When are we going to get to know this Marcus?" Dad asked.

"When you bring the boys up for a game, I guess." My father had already met Marcus last year when he drove him the quick five miles from the campus to the airport, but that was it.

"I might just do that," Dad said, looking determined.

"I would love you to, Dad!" I said excitedly. "Let me know which game you want to come to, and I will get Marcus' free tickets." I loved that my father had just accepted the fact that I had a boyfriend now, and I really loved that he wanted to get to know him. My father was being totally cool about Marcus and me, and I loved him for that.

Saying my farewell to my family, I climbed into the car and started it up. Dad came up to my window, which I rolled down to speak with him. He handed two twenty dollar bills in through the window as he told me to take care of myself. I thanked him and assured him that I would be on guard.

Hopping on the highway, I was soon on my way. I loved the drive to school, probably because I loved the independence of college, and I definitely loved being with Marcus. I missed my friends, but nothing soothed me like Marcus' big cock being fully buried inside me.

Stopping for lunch at Wendy's, I went through the drive-thru and ate in my car with the doors locked. My father had taught me how to protect myself and I was always grateful to him for it. I nonchalantly covered my mark with my hand as I headed inside the fast food restaurant to use the restroom.

I arrived at the university campus by two o'clock and drove directly to Kenan Stadium. By this time, I knew almost every employee of the stadium and every coach, manager, and booster from the football team. So when I unloaded the gift box and a black gym bag from my car, I was confident that I was going to be able to easily be admitted into the stadium no matter who was on security duty.

However, I was wrong. As I approached the nearest gate, there was a security guard in the hut that I did not recognize. I stepped up to the fence and got his attention.

"Hi, I'm Loch. Can you let me in?" I flashed my student ID to him through the voids in the fence.

"What are you here for?" he asked, looking suspiciously over the giant gift box.

"I'm here to see my boyfriend. He's one of the players."

The new security guard bent his knees slightly so that he could get a better look at my face. His eyes focused in on my mark and then he looked into my eyes.

"I'm sorry, sir, but they are in the middle of camp. No

visitors," he said firmly.

"I will not bother them until camp is over. I am going to wait in the locker room for him."

"I'm sorry, sir."

Now I was getting irritated. My whole plan could come to a screeching halt before it even got started if this man didn't let me inside. "Stop calling me *sir* and call your boss. Is it still Stephens?"

He looked shocked for a moment and then answered, "It is."

"Then call him."

The guard picked up a walkie-talkie, pressed a button, and said, "Captain Stephens, come in."

The walkie blared, "Stephens here."

"Cap, I've got a student here who is asking for entrance to the locker room."

"For what purpose?" Stephens asked, his voice sounding irritated. Before the guard could answer, Stephens voice squawked again. "Wait. Is his name Loch?"

The look on the guard's face was priceless. I waved my student ID at him again while nodding my head.

"It is, sir," the guard said.

"Let him in. The team's been waiting for him. He knows where to go."

"Yes, sir." The guard hit a button and the gate clicked and swung open.

"Thanks," I said as I strolled through the gate and kicked it shut behind me.

I made the long walk to the locker room, occasionally passing someone who excitedly called my name. I could hear the players and the coaches on the field. I was tempted to go down one of the ramps and watch them, but I had a limited amount of time to get my surprise set up, and I needed all of it.

The locker room brought back a lot of familiar memories for me when I stepped inside. The smell of body odor, mildew, sweat, and musky testosterone was unforgettable. The UNC locker room had not changed a day since my freshmen year when I was forced to select players to date. I remember that draft day like it was yesterday. I had taken a chance on a shaggy-haired freshman whose name I didn't even know, and he had turned out to be the best thing that had ever happened to me.

Marcus' name was displayed above a locker in the prominent center area of the room. I knew that this area was usually reserved for seniors, but there must have been extra lockers that were assigned to juniors who were standouts. There were four sections of lockers that formed a square with the standard wooden benches in front of them. The middle of the square was just an empty carpeted area where the coach could stand and see most of the players.

Glad that the locker room was empty, I went to Marcus' locker and put my stuff down on the wooden bench in front of it. I could not resist the urge to go to his locker, stick my head inside, and breathe in deeply. Marcus Battle's smell was something that I never had been able to pass up. My cock got hard instantly as his musk filled my nostrils.

Unzipping my gym bag, I quickly pulled out several black straps, shortened versions of the type used to tie down items in the backs of their pickups.

I lifted the lid off the box and watched as its four sides collapsed until there was just a flat piece of heavy cardboard in the shape of a cross on the bench. The top of the box had a big Carolina blue bow and a gift tag that read,

To Marcus Battle
Congrats on another successful completion of football camp.
From Your Number One Fan

Smiling to myself, I knelt on the thick carpet and ran one of the straps through two slits in the bottom of the box and around the wooden bench. I pulled the strap tight as I fastened it into place. This would assure that the box did not fall or get knocked off the bench.

I quickly stripped off my clothes and put on a jock strap that I had made from one of Marcus' old practice jerseys. It barely covered anything, but it outlined my ass beautifully as his number covered my cock and balls. After folding my clothes, I put them into my gym bag and threw it into the bottom of his locker. Sitting down on the bench, I attached two black restraints in the shape of figure eights to my ankles. Both of my ankles were secured, and an empty loop hung from each.

I walked over to a rolling rack and grabbed two towels from it. I folded them both, putting one under the bench and the other on top of the box. Checking the clock on the wall, I figured that I was right on time. I didn't want to start too soon, since I would be forced to stay in the same position for a very long time.

Thank God for those patience lessons that Mr. Lewellyn had taught me!

There was a thin string attached to each side of the box. These were gathered into the middle of the box, with a wooden bead holding all of them together. I lay down on my back on top of the box, slipped under the strings, and strapped my chest and waist to the strap that was already around the bench. Having practiced this several times at home, I knew that I could successfully bind myself, but I had to remain calm in order to get it done on time.

Once I was firmly strapped to the bench, I reached down and grabbed the box lid. I held it between my legs as I reached for the wooden bead that was on my stomach. I pulled on the bead, and slowly all four walls of the box rose back into place. I had to raise my feet and legs into the air so the box would close.

The box lid had a handle on the inside, so I easily lifted it out of the box and then onto the four walls. The box lid held the box together so that I could drop the strings holding up the walls.

Now for the hard part!

I strapped a gag onto my face. It was an unusual gag, because it basically held my lips and mouth open instead of closed. Mr. Lewellyn had told me that it was for people who were opposed to giving blow jobs. This gag basically gave them no choice in the matter. I was not opposed to giving Marcus a blow job, but was using it for the visual effect. I had decided not to blindfold myself, since I desperately wanted to watch my muscled behemoth boyfriend when he unwrapped his present and when he destroyed my ass shortly after.

Unfortunately, the decision not to blind myself was going to cause me to have to see Marcus' team and coaching staff's faces as they watched the entire event. It would be super embarrassing, but I was committed to it, so there was no turning back.

Raising my arms, I slipped each of my wrists into the loose loops hooked to my ankles, and, using a lot of ab strength, I raised my upper body momentarily. Using my teeth, I tightened the extended cords on my wrists, pinning them to my ankles.

Relaxing once I was completely bound, I felt myself sweating from the exertion and the hot confines of the box. Even though my arms and legs were lifted together towards the box lid, I could relax into the bonds and get a little relief.

Now, all I had to do was wait.

CHAPTER NINE

I heard the managers first and then came the seniors. The box only muffled their voices, but I could hear their comments easily.

"Oh, shit!"

"Looks like Battle got a present!"

"It's a fucking huge present."

"I want a present that I get to fuck like that."

"Whatever it is, it's not as good as last year's present!"

"Battle tore that ass up last year, no wonder he's not getting that again. Loch probably couldn't walk for a week after that."

I was grateful for Mr. Lewellyn's training. Being able to stay absolutely still was a real bonus in this situation. Suddenly I felt a tingling sensation run over my skin, and I knew Marcus was close.

The players and managers grew very excited as Marcus must have appeared in the locker room. "Oh, shit! Here he comes!"

"What the fuck?" Marcus' deep voice resonated inside the box and turned me on like nothing else could. I felt all warm and gooey inside like I hadn't seen him for years when it had been hardly two months.

"You got a present, Battle," someone said.

"Read the tag," someone else said.

I heard him scrape the top of the box as he looked at the tag. My body was ringing like a bell with sexual energy.

"Who's it from, Battle?"

His deep voice boomed as he asked, "Where is Loch?"

My whole mindset suddenly changed. With that one question I knew that he was worried about me. I just assumed that he would open the present right away and find me.

"I don't know," someone said quickly.

"Has anyone seen him," Marcus asked. "He was supposed to be here."

"We haven't seen him, Battle. Maybe there's something in the present that tells you where he is . . ."

"Maybe," he said. His voice was louder now, so I imagined him to be looking at the present.

The lid of the box started to move and then the whole box shook as he worked the lid off. My heart threatened to pound out of my chest. In an instant, the lid was off and the sides of the box collapsed right on cue.

I had been in the dark for a while, so I blinked my eyes to quickly readjust them to the blinding light. The locker room was silent as a tomb except for the clatter of the sides of the box as they came to rest.

"Loch," Marcus' voice called in the huskiest, most luscious tone that I had ever heard.

"Holy fuck!" one of the players said with a voice of awe.

"Battle is the luckiest fuck in the whole world!" another one exclaimed.

"Now, that's a present anyone would like," yet another player said.

Finally, I was able to focus in on my boyfriend. I had not seen him in two months, and he was glorious. He towered over me, of course, as I lay folded and strapped onto the bench, but he was bigger than before. I knew every inch of his body, and I could see that his biceps were bigger and his chest looked broader.

Marcus was dirty from the day's play, but I could see under the dirt that his copper beard was fuller than last school year and he had his hair cut short. His eyes glittered at me with fire and excitement.

His smell was amazing—sweat and musk combining to overwhelm my senses. I could feel my draw to him just like every other time I had been in his presence. It was unrelenting and supernatural in its intensity.

Some player yelled out, "Shit! Battle is getting ready to tear that father-fucking hole up!"

"Loch better watch out!" someone else added before bursting into laughter.

"I think that marked guy knows exactly what he is doing," someone else said.

Besides his initial saying of my name when the box flew open, Marcus had remained silent. Moving around to my head, he suddenly lifted a massive leg and straddled the bench that I was strapped onto.

My eyes were full of his hugeness as he towered above me. I watched without breathing as he moved his dirty hands to the front of his crotch. Untying the front laces of his football pants, Marcus pulled a huge erection out of his fly. He held onto the locker with one hand as he pointed that magnificent cock downwards into my mouth with the other.

My boyfriend's huge cock was soon between my lips, and the taste of him was divine. His musky smell was even more intense in his crotch, and it got closer and closer to my nose as he lowered his legs. Each inch he squatted sent another inch of his man-meat further into my mouth and throat.

Marcus moaned as I wrapped as much of my lips as the gag allowed around his big member and used my tongue to lick all the surface area of his sensitive skin. Reaching down, my boyfriend pulled on the leather thong holding the gag in place and ripped it off my head. He threw it to the side. The giant cockhead on his big dick started to leak a steady stream of delicious man-goo that I now slurped and sucked with wild abandon.

That large unit stretched my lips wide as he dipped it repeatedly into my hungry hole. Marcus' breathing started to change — getting shallower and faster. He was close to his climax, so I wasn't surprised when he pulled out of my mouth and settled between my legs.

Straddling the bench again, but not my body this time, Marcus slowly entered my exposed hole with nothing but the spit shine that I had given him as lube. He kept his dark-eyed gaze trained on me as he pushed his giant cock head against my puckered hole. I whined, not because he was hurting me, but because he was going so slowly, causing my hole to push in on itself instead of allowing him entrance.

My football playing boyfriend soon rectified the situation by continuing to push himself into me. I released a huge breath I had been unconsciously holding as he finally punched through and slid into me. His cock deliciously filled me up as my stretched ass hole squeezed his thick shaft from the head all the way down to the root.

There was nothing like being filled by Marcus Battle. It was the most unbelievable feeling in the world. I craved it when I didn't have it and lived for it when I did. I tried to push my ass back against him to make sure that every possible inch of him was drilling into me. Having my legs up and together gave me an even tighter hole.

"Fuck!" I groaned with my mouth still feeling forced open by the spreader even though it was long gone. My eyelids felt like they wanted to close all by themselves, but my will wouldn't let them. I wanted to see everything.

Marcus slow-fucked me, punching my prostate over and over. I loved being in this position where I could watch my boyfriend tearing my ass up. My arms and legs were starting to feel the strain of being bound above me, but I didn't care as long as that huge dong was drilling the shit out of me.

As he pulled off his practice jersey, I could see on Marcus' face that he was really enjoying this fuck. Our connection seemed to be intact, as if the summer separation had never happened. Even though it was the start of our third year together, I was just as hot for him as I had ever been and he seemed to feel the same way towards me.

Feeling my climax building, I could also feel the same thing happening to Marcus. I was squeezing his big joint with each out-thrust, and I could feel it swell and throb inside me. I continued to sweat under the strain and Marcus was soon shiny with perspiration as well.

I wanted to touch him and lick him all over, but I had to be patient. Marcus and I reached our climax at the same time — he flooded my ass with his scalding hot cum as I shot mine across my sweaty chest and watched it run off. Marcus continued to fuck me, thrusting into me deeply even as his body spasmed with his explosion.

Never had I been more impressed with his stamina than I was in this moment. Marcus Battle continued to try to saw my ass in half as he built towards a second climax. This time he fucked me with speed and power.

Suddenly I became aware of the rest of the world. I saw the other players watching us fuck and heard their crude comments. I saw the freshmen players and coaches who had just arrived inside the locker room getting their first look at the present that Marcus had received.

Marcus' fast hard pounding of my ass caused a whole host of comments to be said from the others in the locker room.

"God damn! Look at Battle fuck that hole."

"I'm surprised they aren't catching fire."

"How the fuck did he get so lucky?"

"You've seen how fucking big his cock is, haven't you?"

"If this is how they are when they are happy to see each other, I'd hate to see Battle angry fuck."

"Loch better put his ass in the ice bath after Battle gets

finished with him."

"I've never seen anything like this before."

A deeper, more mature male voice said, "Let's give them some privacy, huh, guys?"

That last comment seemed to clear out the crowd, and we were soon left virtually alone as the other players cleaned up and headed home for the rest of the summer. I'm not sure Marcus even noticed as he pounded me over and over. I was so glad that I had thought to put that folded towel down under me for padding. Marcus, in contrast, was totally focused on me, and I admired his attention to detail.

When Marcus came this time, it was with a primal yell. He arched his back and threw back his head as he groaned at one end and erupted into my sore ass at the other. He was amazing, and I was in total awe of him. I felt like we had never been apart, but had stayed connected the entire summer. He fucked me like no one else in the whole world ever had, and I felt like I was the luckiest marked man in the world.

Returning back to himself after his climax, Marcus finally looked down at me and said, "Hi, Loch."

"Hi, Marcus," I said, suddenly very shy.

"I obviously missed you," he said with a small smile, revealing beautiful white teeth.

"Me, too," I admitted, blushing.

"This was a nice surprise," he said, indicating the gift box with his eyes.

"Thanks. I didn't mean to make you panicky when you didn't see me." That result was not something that I had even considered as a possibility, and I chided myself for being foolish not to think of it.

He blinked his beautiful hazel eyes and said, "I was just worried."

"I know. I appreciate it." I couldn't help but smile up at him. He had protected me from the very beginning—refusing to use me like his teammates, saving me from a nasty situation with one of my dates, always looking out for my safety and best interests.

"Wanna shower with me?" he asked innocently.

I was very aware that Marcus' huge phallus was still inside of me. "Absolutely!"

He smirked at me and said, "I'm not sure that I'm ready to give up this easy access that you have going on here though . . ."

"You don't have to," I said with a raised eyebrow. I had considered this scenario and was ready for it.

"Oh yeah?" he challenged me.

"Just unhook the straps around my waist and chest."

I watched as he did, and my feeling of being securely bound to the bench was soon replaced with the relief of re-lease. That was shortly followed by the unsteadiness of my knowledge that I was now able to fall off the bench.

As if he could read my thoughts and emotions, Marcus smirked at me and said, "I got you."

"You always do," I agreed with him in a huskier voice than usual.

How in the hell could I be still burning for him when he had just thoroughly fucked me twice and his cock was still thrumming away deep inside of me?

Marcus reached down and rubbed my chest. I got a good view of his magnificent chest, wishing that I could run my hands over it. He had a little more chest hair than last year and it seemed to be a deeper copper color than before. Licking my lips in anticipation of being able to suck on all his body parts, I watched as he pushed his football pants and jock strap down to the floor and stepped out of them.

"I think I want these free also," Marcus said almost absent-mindedly as he unsnapped my ankle restraints. "Put them around my waist," he commanded.

Fuck! Marcus using his Master voice was just icing on the cake.

My cock began to harden again with his command of me and I followed his direction, even though my leg muscles protested. I resisted the urge to lower my legs and stretch them out. My legs were long, which was the only way that I could circle Marcus' thick waist and hook my feet together behind him.

With the release of my feet, my arms were the only things bound together, and I wanted so desperately to lower them. Marcus helped me with that dilemma by lowering his head and sticking it through the space between my arms. My arms were now around his thick neck, and our faces were dangerously close to each other.

"I like this," I said to break the tension.

"Do you, now?" He smirked.

I rubbed the short hairs on the back of his head with my fingers and added, "I like your new haircut also."

He smiled. "It's really short for me."

"Looks great with your new body." I literally salivated.

"Thanks. I see that you have put on some muscle over the summer as well."

"There's only one muscle that matters to me right now, Marcus." I moaned as my cock hardened to a painful state.

Marcus lowered his lips to my ear and said, "I want you to be silent now, Loch." His voice carried the promise of great pleasure if I followed his orders.

"Yes, Master," I answered firmly.

Marcus growled from deep inside his chest at my use of the title that neither of us took lightly. With one swift movement, he stood up, pulling me with him. I slid down his pole against his crotch as he let me settle against him. He carried me with all the practiced ease of a father with a baby and headed towards the showers.

I lay my head on my boyfriend's broad shoulder and reveled in the sensation of his bearded face occasionally scraping my neck or face as he walked. I could feel his heart beating inside his massive chest, but his pulse never seemed to quicken, even while carrying me.

We reached the showers, and Marcus turned on two that were beside each other and adjusted them until they were the right temperature. He held us under the water, letting it wash the sweat, dirt, and cum off of both of us. I thought we would get cleaned up, but Marcus had other plans.

With a firm move, he pushed my back against the tiled wall and began to fuck me again. He rutted my ass by stabbing upward into me repeatedly until we both came again. The close contact friction of my cock and his hairy stomach had been too much for me and I reached my climax moments before he did.

"Fuck! There it is." He groaned as my ass muscles tightened around his thick shaft with my climax. "Let me have all of that tight hole, Loch."

I remained silent like I had been commanded, but I wanted to tell him how much he meant to me and how I give all of myself to him each time we fucked. Having to rest on the fact that he already knew this information, I crumpled onto his shoulder as he fell over the edge of his climax and pumped more semen into me.

Feeling cum start to sluice out of my sloppy ass, I was glad that we were in the shower where it was okay to make such a mess. Marcus pressed his whole body against me and took deep heaving breaths as he tried to regain his composure.

"I can't wait until we can just be quiet and fuck in our favorite position," he said gently.

I was stunned by his sensitive side and smiled into his neck. I pushed my lips out and made contact with a thick vein that was popping out on his neck and kissed it. Shifting in his arms, I kissed more places on his neck and then started to suck and lick his delicious skin as well.

"Haven't had enough yet, Loch?" he asked in almost a whisper.

This was a question, so I was allowed to answer it. "I can never get enough of you, Master."

He grunted and then lustfully said, "You are just asking for it now, Loch."

"No, I am demanding it, Master."

CHAPTER TEN

"I have a surprise for you," Marcus told me as we finished dressing in the locker room. He had finally let me off his big cock, and now my ass was missing him something fierce. My anal ring was still clutching for his thick rod even though it had been removed.

"Do you now?" I asked, using his new favorite phrase. I was dressed, but still moving very gingerly.

"I do," he said, his face completely animated with excitement. "Did I hurt you, Loch?" he suddenly asked as he saw my awkward movement.

"Yes, but in a way that I needed to be hurt so badly," I replied. I knew he would not forgive himself if he hurt me and probably would refuse to fuck me again today, so I had to reassure him.

"You sure?" he asked, his large forehead already creased with worry lines.

"I'm sure, you big lug. You gave me just what I needed."

We walked out of the empty stadium to the parking lot in silence that was not the least bit awkward. Marcus looked at my car and said, "You wanna follow me?"

"You have a car?" I asked.

He pointed at a black pick-up and said, "Dad bought me a truck." He was grinning from ear-to-ear.

"Awesome!" I said. "Can't wait to ride you in that . . . I mean ride in that," I said flirtatiously.

He laughed easily and said, "Yes!"

"I'll follow you. We going to your dorm?"

"Not today, Loch, not today," he smirked, using one of our pet phrases from freshman year.

I jumped in my car and followed the black truck as Marcus drove off the campus and then pulled into the driveway of a brick house on a small piece of property. He stopped the truck and I pulled up to the house beside him.

"What do you think?" he asked as he waited for me to approach the door.

"Whose house is this?"

"It's ours!"

"Really?" I asked in shock.

"You said that you wanted to room with me this year . . ."

"And you always give me what I need . . ."

He cracked a broad grin and said, "Always."

"A football booster gave you this house?" I asked as Marcus unlocked the door and stepped inside. I couldn't believe how close to campus we were, but totally private at the same time. I could walk to some of my classes from this house.

"He's letting us rent it for pretty cheap."

Once inside, I saw that it was a much bigger house than it looked from the outside. The floorplan was open and had recently been remodeled. It was perfect.

Marcus said, "C'mon and I will show you the bedroom." He took off towards the second floor. I followed, taking in everything. "There are three bedrooms and a bathroom up here." He indicated the first room, "This is Jordan's room."

"Ah, we have roommates," I said, piecing together the puzzle of this big house. Jordan was Marcus' roommate from his dorm and a member of the football team. "Vance living with us also?"

"Yep. This is his room," Marcus said, indicating the second bedroom. Vance was another friend and football player. I had spent Spring Break with Marcus, Vance, and Jordan the last two years. We got along great and I loved that we were all going to be living together.

"So, this must be our room," I said, looking in the third bedroom, frowning at the same twin-sized bed inside.

"No, that one is Finn's."

My head snapped back to look at Marcus, who was grinning.

"You like him, don't you?" Marcus carefully asked.

"Finn Bryant from your team?" I asked.

"Yes."

Finn was a redshirt junior player. One year older than the rest of us, but in the same grade. He was a quarterback who was tall and thin. I didn't remember seeing him when I had to pick a boyfriend in the football dating contest where I found Marcus, but I did remember Marcus mentioning him a few times last year. I knew from the media guide that he was a redhead, but that was all I knew about him.

"He's a friend of yours?" I asked Marcus.

"Yes."

"Then he must be a good person. I'm sure I will like him." Changing the subject abruptly, I asked, "Where are we sleeping?"

"Your bedroom is down here," he said as he headed back to the first floor.

"My bedroom?" I asked on the verge of outrage.

Marcus showed me to the master bedroom—a large room with lots of windows, a king-sized bed, and its own bathroom. It smelled like Marcus, and I breathed in deeply of its musky masculine stench. "Our bedroom," he corrected himself.

I looked at my big man with wide eyes and a lump in my throat. "Do you mean that I'm going to get to sleep with you every night?"

"Of course. Isn't that what you wanted?"

"Yes, but I didn't think you would agree to it. I am your

number one distraction, according to you."

He smiled and said, "You still are, but I'm going to give this a shot . . . with rules, of course."

"Of course," I conceded as I took a seat on the edge of the bed. "You want to hash those out now?"

"Sure. We can break in the new bed, move your shit in, and then go out to eat."

"Sounds like a plan," I said with excitement. "Are the boys staying around or going home?" School didn't officially start for three more weeks.

"Finn is staying and working out with me, but Vance and Jordan have already left for home."

"Cool. So, Mr. Battle, what can I do for you today to thank you for this wonderful surprise you have given me?"

His face lit up with delight and desire. "I want to feel your lips around my cock and then maybe we can use those wrist restraints again."

"You mean these?" I asked, as I slowly pulled the figure eight restraints from my shorts pockets.

"Yes, those," he said gruffly.

"I thought we might have need of them again," I said with a hint of mischief. I rose from the bed, stepped out of my clothes quickly, and knelt on the carpet.

Marcus stripped and sat down on the bed beside me. He tousled my hair as I reached out for his big prick.

Right before I sucked him into my mouth, I looked up at my boyfriend and said, "Thanks for this, Marcus. It means a lot to me."

"Welcome. You belong to me," he said, growling.

"And you belong to me," I said lustfully as I opened my jaw and swallowed him.

Marcus' cock was hot and tasted clean, like the soap from the shower in the locker room. I let him punch into the back of my throat before I pulled off him, turned my head to the side, and slid my lips up and down the outside of his shaft like he was an ear of corn.

Marcus immediately began to leak his delicious self-lube, which I slurped down without hesitation. Using my tongue as a scoop, I dug in his piss hole trying to retrieve as much of it as I could. The object of my constant desire was showing me why he was a god next to all of the rest of us mortals. He had just come three times less than an hour ago, but now he was ready to go again. Marcus Battle was amazing.

"I think you have gotten so much better at that." He groaned at me as I looked up his chest to his face while his thick horse cock was inside my mouth, spreading my lips far apart.

Pulling off of him, I said, "I aim to please, Master." I started sucking so hard that my cheeks hollowed out as I worked all the way up that long tube.

He chuckled. "And please, you do!" He grabbed my face between his meaty hands and began to fuck it with more than a little bit of energy and force. Marcus obviously enjoyed dominating me and I was more than willing to let him.

When he reached his climax, he let go of my face and held the back of my head down onto his throbbing meat missile. I let his fat cock head punch into my throat and held my breath as he lost control and exploded straight down into my stomach. Hot thick cum shot out of his cock and ran right down my esophagus. I pulled back off him so that I could taste his sweet cream before it all went to waste down my throat.

Marcus' cum tasted so good that I never could get enough. I tried to coax more of his creamy spunk from that fuck pole, pumping his shaft with my hands, my thumb pressing on the bottom vein and my tongue trying to dig more out of his cum vent. I was rewarded with a few more translucent pearls that I held on my tongue for him to see before I swallowed them.

"Jesus." He groaned quietly. He pulled me up onto the bed

and said, "How about we start every day with that?"

So, the negotiations of the rules have begun.

"I will be glad to do that for you, sir."

His hooded eyes suddenly opened wider at my use of the formal pronoun. "And what would you like in return, Loch?"

"I can't really think straight without your big cock being buried inside me, so let's do that first and then I will think about it," I said, teasing him.

He growled like a big copper bear and began to strip off his clothes. I was soon on my back on the bed. Loving that the bed smelled so much like my boyfriend, I took deep inhalations of his scent and filled my nostrils with it.

"Put your hands together, Loch." Marcus had slipped into Master-mode, which excited me beyond belief. I instantly felt the familiar twinge of excitement in my balls.

I did as I was told and hungrily watched as my boyfriend strapped the wrist restraints onto my arms again. He smiled down at me when my hands were thoroughly bound. I licked my lips in anticipation of being under his massive frame yet again.

But Marcus had other ideas. "It is only fitting that we break in the new place with the position that broke us in," he said with a serious face.

I nodded my head in understanding, sat on my knees, and motioned for him to lie down on the bed beside me with my bound hands. Marcus followed my suggestion and lay down, propping himself up on the pillows. I loved the fact that he was sentimental and that I had come to terms with the cons for this sexual position which we had come to be possessive of.

Marcus reached out a long arm, captured a bottle of lube from the nightstand, and pumped some into my folded hands. I used it immediately to give him a nice tug-and-pull as Marcus hardened in my hand within seconds. It was awkward to give him a hand job when my wrists were restrained together, but I think we both quite enjoyed it.

Now it was my turn to be sentimental. "Don't you ever get tired of me, Battle?"

Marcus laughed out loud. "We've been reunited for like what, two hours? And I have fucked you three times and shot another load down your throat. That doesn't sound like someone who is ever going to get tired of you."

"I know, but I worry that—"

"But nothing! You have nothing to worry about. I'm the one who can be replaced easily. If I lose you . . ." Whatever he was thinking or imagining was too terrible for him to continue.

"You have nothing to worry about!" I threw back at him. "I'm addicted to you." I could feel myself starting to blush. I could let him fuck me in every hole, sit there holding his throbbing member in my lubed hand, and swallow gallons of his cum, but telling him how much he meant to me was hard.

"And I'm addicted to you," he said simply. "Now get down here on my cock."

"Yes, sir." My voice was so husky with lust and desire that I hardly recognized it.

Since I didn't have much use of my hands, Marcus had to guide me slowly down onto his flagpole as he held it upright. It was a little acrobatic, but I trusted my body in Marcus' big mitts more than anywhere else in the world. He pushed his thick stormtrooper-shaped cock head into my sore hole and then slowly pulled my hips down until I was completely impaled on his big rod and I was sitting firmly on his crotch.

"Yes, sir," Marcus sighed, repeating my words. He thrust his hips forward several times, sending his prong up into me while he held me still above him.

I grunted my pleasure to him, knowing that it was important to remain quiet. Reveling in the fact that every nerve ending in my body was sending screaming messages to the pleasure center of my brain, I bowed my head, put my bound hands above my head, and spread my fingers out in a sign of supplication.

Marcus slowly pulled me down by one shoulder to lie flat on his big chest. His legs wrapped around mine and then his feet hooked them in place. This was our position — one we had perfected two years ago and which we enjoyed as much for the memories as for the quiet pleasure that we both got from it.

CHAPTER ELEVEN

I lay quietly on Marcus' chest and listened to his heart beat against my back. His huge cock throbbed away inside of my ass and I was right where I needed to be.

Is it possible to spend the rest of my two years of college right here?

Marcus slowly ran his hands up from my hips and along my sides. I loved that he was no longer afraid or unwilling to touch me. He had definitely grown during the length of our relationship, and I was extremely satisfied with him. His hands were warm and rough as he caressed my skin.

He explored my body with his fingertips — pinching my nipples, exploring the hollow areas at the top of my hips, and even touching my sensitive prick. My cock jumped at his touch. Marcus wrapped a hand around my neck and another one around my hardening cock. He spit on his hand holding my cock and returned to start pumping my hard shaft.

I moaned in response to his hand job and was rewarded by Marcus moving his hand up to my face. A big thumb snaked its way into my mouth and hooked into the corner between my lips. I sucked on his thick digit as my climax built.

Enjoying a myriad of sensations, I arched my back and shot a volley of hot semen ropes across my chest and stomach. Marcus' thumb in my mouth, his cock throbbing away deep inside my ass, and his insistent hand moving like a piston up and down my dick were just too much stimulation to take.

My ass muscles caved in around my boyfriend's thick phallus that was buried to the hilt inside of me, gripping him with so much pressure that I thought I could feel each and every vein standing up on his hard shaft. He was a marble statue that my flesh had grown around, neither able to extricate itself from the other.

"There it is," Marcus whispered into my ear. I knew that he was waiting for the moment when my climax gave him the ultimate tight hole to plunder, and I was more than happy to give it to him.

Marcus happily began to fuck me with long deep thrusts that threatened to unsettle me from the top of his body. He was always able to reach places inside me that no one else even came close to. Marcus picked up his pace, grabbed both of my legs, lifted them up and back, and was soon tearing me up from below.

My asshole was burning already, but now it was just a roaring wildfire that threatened to make me combust in an explosion of brightly colored sparks. No one fucked me like Marcus Battle, and no one made me feel the heady combination of pleasure and pain like he did.

My footballer grunted loudly as he released another load of hot man-goo inside me. He continued to thrust into me right through his climax, sluicing his hot sauce out of me.

I released whatever tension I had left in my body and melted into him. "Marcus," I said dreamily.

"Loch," he responded to me hoarsely. He reached up, released my hands, and slid me off of him to the side. "Want to take a nap?"

"Yes," I said, already shutting my eyes.

"Me, too," he said as he pulled the sheet up to cover us, lying down beside me.

I woke up an hour or so later. Marcus was already out of bed and I could smell meat cooking on a grill. Gingerly, I made my way to the bathroom, feeling every little move deep inside my ass. I got cleaned up, which included a very long, very hot shower. Wanting to soak in a hot tub, I chose not to because I wanted to be with Marcus more than I wanted my ass to stop hurting.

Once I felt better, I dried off and discovered that my laundry baskets of clothes had been brought into the bedroom. I grabbed a pair of clean shorts and a t-shirt and headed out to look for Marcus.

I found him in the back yard. He was grilling and looking very manly doing it. I saw that he had a beer, so I made my way to the kitchen, grabbed two more and made my way out to the back yard. As I got closer, I thought I heard him talking and assumed he was on the phone. Very unethically of me, I slowed down and listened at the screen door.

Marcus' voice projected, "He's quite possibly the best thing that ever happened to me."

"You mean him picking you?" This voice was not on the phone but in the actual back yard. It shocked me, because I thought we were alone. I didn't recognize who it was.

"Well, yes, but not just that. Loch has . . . changed me."

"Changed you?"

"Yeah. He's made me into something that I don't think I would be without him."

"Like a freaking sex machine?" the other voice asked with a chuckle.

"No, like the man I am now was just lying dormant in there. I feel like there were several different versions of me . . . possibilities of what I could become inside of me, and he saw them, picked the one that both he and I wanted the most, and made me into it."

"That's deep, man."

"I know," Marcus said with a laugh. "I know that it sounds strange, but I think Loch could see something inside of me and he has worked to bring it out."

"And he what . . . made you become it?" the disembodied voice asked in disbelief.

"Yes! That's exactly what he did," Marcus said, turning his head from the grill and nodding to the stranger that I still couldn't see.

"How's that even possible?" The other voice sounded incredulous.

"I don't know," Marcus said, turning back to the food on the grill. "Just like I don't know how we have the connection that we do." He paused for a second and then said, "Like I can feel that he is near me now, probably standing at the back door, even though I can't see him."

Busted! I forgot about our freaking Spidey sense for each other!

I reached for the door handle as I saw Marcus turn towards the door and also saw the owner of the other voice lean forward and look my way. Stepping through the open door and closing it behind me, I held up the beers and asked, "Anyone need a fresh one?"

The stranger was Finn, our new roommate, although I barely recognized him, because his head had been completely shaved.

"I see the advantages of him already," Finn said, putting down his bottle and reaching for the one I held out.

"Thanks, Loch," Marcus said, grabbing the other one and ignoring Finn's comment. "You didn't get one for yourself?" he asked. I loved that he noticed little things like that and was always looking out for me.

"I did, but I didn't realize that you had company," I said to him as I turned to Finn.

"Oh," he said, realizing now what had happened. "You remember Finn, right?"

"I do," I said as I stepped towards the older football player. Putting my hand on his shiny dome and rubbing, I added, "But I don't remember this." He was only slightly taller than me.

They both laughed, Marcus easily and Finn nervously. I was affecting him with my physical presence.

Good information to know . . .

"I started shaving it at the beginning of the summer. You like it, Loch?" he asked, hope shining in his eyes.

"I'm not sure," I said as I removed my hand from his head and put it on my chin like I was thinking. "We'll have to see."

They both chuckled, and Marcus informed me that Finn generally did not like body hair. "The team has been kidding him about it for years."

"Oh, yeah?" I asked. "Are you shaved all over?" I asked as I ran a finger down his substantial chest to his crotch. I knew that I was provoking him sexually, but I just couldn't resist.

He swallowed hard and said, "Yes."

"Interesting," I commented as I turned on heel and went to see what Marcus was grilling. "I hope you're not expecting me to clean the shower after you shave all that hair off all the time."

We all laughed.

Dinner turned out to be burgers and hot dogs. Finn was almost as big as Marcus, and they both had worked out hard today. As a result, they consumed a tremendous amount of food. I enjoyed talking to Finn and getting to know him better. He was very likable, and the three of us were soon fast friends.

I stood up from the table, grabbing the condiments and heading to the fridge. I watched over my shoulder as Finn's focus was glued to my ass.

"So, Battle, how does this thing with Loch work?" Finn asked, a little too quickly.

"What thing with Loch?" Marcus asked, stone-faced.

"You know . . . with him being here with us and you two being a thing and the rest of us . . ."

"Are you under the impression that I'm going to share Loch with you?" Marcus' voice was still very neutral. I had stopped moving now and was watching this scene unfold in front of me.

"Won't you?" Finn asked in disbelief.

Marcus' voice was impassioned when he finally spoke. "Loch is not my property. He is not a Servant who I can command to fuck my friends. He is his own person." I watched as Marcus slowly turned his eyes from Finn to focus on me. They laser-locked onto mine as he continued, "Loch knows that if he wants to fuck around with someone, he can ask me. He also knows that if I want him to fuck around with someone that I will ask, but he has the ability to decide for himself."

I smiled as I realized that Marcus Battle was not giving up any control over me, even as he preached on how much independence and free-will I had. That made me hotter than anything else he had said, because in the end I wanted nothing more than to belong to him, be dominated by him, and be totally at his beck and call.

Finn tried to justify his line of logic. "I just thought since he has fucked with Jordan and Vance already . . ."

"Loch, speak," Marcus ordered me.

"I think Finn has a good point, Marcus. We can't very well hang out constantly with that hanging over our heads."

"True," Marcus agreed, seeing the sense in my logic.

I regarded Finn for a couple of seconds. "But, it's not going to be tonight, Finn, or probably not for a few days. I need to get to know you better, and Marcus has a lot of nut-juice stored up from the long summer without me that I need to drain from his beautiful balls."

"Fuck me," Finn said under his breath as he stared at both of us with wide eyes.

Marcus and I burst out laughing. "You're gonna have to get used to that, Bryant. Loch doesn't pull any punches when he speaks," Marcus told him.

"And it will only be rare occasions, Finn. My ass belongs to

Battle, and he will be the only one who gets it on a regular basis. You understand?" I asked him.

"Yes," he said.

"Unfortunately for you, living with Loch is going to give you more blue balls than anything else," Marcus told him. "The guys on the team are going to assume that you're hitting it every day, but it's not going to be like that."

"I'll deal," Finn said. "I will live for the moments when I get to experience the Loch phenomena . . ."

"Wow!" I said. "I didn't know that I was a *phenomenon*."

"Well, you are," Marcus said flatly.

"You guys want to watch a movie?" Finn asked, changing the subject.

I looked at Marcus. We didn't need words to communicate with each other. We were always on the same page, so I wasn't surprised with his answer when he spoke.

"Not tonight, Finn. I'm going to go to bed and show Loch what he's been missing for the past two months."

I smirked and nodded slightly while looking at Finn's shocked face.

Finn recovered enough to say, "You guys banged it out in the locker room, and I could smell sex when I came home this afternoon . . ."

"What's your point, Finn?" I asked with a snort.

Finn's shoulders slumped and he admitted, "I guess I don't have one. If Loch was mine, I would probably spend every waking minute fucking him also."

"Aw, only the waking ones?" I teased Finn.

Marcus laughed so hard that he had to hold his stomach. I grabbed two bottles of water from the fridge and said, "Night, Finn."

Marcus said, "See you tomorrow, buddy."

"We still playing golf tomorrow, Marcus?"

"Of course. Wake me when you're ready, if I'm not up."

I didn't hear Finn's response, since I was back in the bedroom by this time. I stripped off my clothes quickly and climbed onto the big bed.

"Anxious?" Marcus asked quietly when he saw me, after he had locked the bedroom door.

"Always," I said laughing. I had no shame where he was concerned.

Marcus undressed, grabbed my legs, and spun me around. He pulled my shoulders towards the end of the bed until my head hung over the mattress. I knew what that meant, and I was more than ready to comply. Closing my eyes, I opened my mouth and waited.

The man I considered my Master didn't immediately thrust his cock in my mouth, much to my surprise. I opened my eyes, suddenly alert for any potential problem. Marcus stood over me, looking down at me, but not into my eyes. Looking down quickly, I tried to see where he was looking.

In a moment of unexpected tenderness, Marcus reached down and touched my neck. He ran one long finger along a vein on my neck, from the small hollow at the top of my ribcage to my chin.

"You are an amazing man, Loch," Marcus said, his voice sounding far away.

I almost snorted when I asked, "Why do you say that?"

"Because you are," he answered, as he used his whole hand to stroke my neck. "You saw something in me that I'm not sure that I even saw in myself. It wasn't enough for you to just see it, but you have brought it out of me. You're the catalyst that has allowed me to become the man you knew I could be."

Opening my lips, I started to say something, but Marcus pinched my lips together and then stroked my cheek with the backs of his knuckles.

He continued, "I just want you to know that I give you all the credit, Loch. You have changed my life." There was such a note of sincerity to his voice that it gave me pause for a few moments.

I wanted to tell him that he had done the same thing for me, but I knew it meant more for me to follow his command than to say it. Marcus Battle was a unique man who constantly amazed me with his compassion and thoughtfulness towards me. He was nothing like most of the NOMARs I had encountered in my short life, so I thanked my lucky stars every day for finding him.

Seeming to snap back from wherever he was, Marcus gazed at me and said, "I can see that you are struggling not to talk, Loch," he said, smirking at me. "Let's see if this helps." Marcus placed his bulbous cock head against my lips.

I kept his cock head there, but let my tongue slide through my lips and onto the super-soft skin of his cock head. Rewarded with his quick gasp, I continued to lick him and then opened wide, swallowing his lap-hog into my hungry hole.

Marcus placed both of his palms on the top of my chest, leaned forward, and guided his extra-large joint into my open mouth. He completely filled my hole and started to knock on my throat before his balls were sitting on my eyes.

Moaning my happiness to him, I reached up, grabbed both of his ass cheeks by the dimples, and pulled him into my throat.

"God damn!" Marcus groaned as he bent his knees and plunged into the small pipe leading to my stomach.

Pulling back to let me breathe, Marcus put his weight onto his arms and proceeded to fuck my face like he had missed me for the past two months. I concentrated on keeping my teeth out of the way while he repeatedly invaded my mouth, leaking enough pre-cum to cause me to over-salivate.

"Fuck!" Marcus groaned out the word as he ran his hands down my chest, pinched my nipples hard, and reached his climax. He flooded my mouth with salty nut-juice that ran out of both sides of my grin.

I sucked, swallowed, and licked that monster tool that was such a great part of who Marcus Battle was until he came back to his self. He extracted his dick from me and spun me around on the bed so that my head wasn't hanging over the side. I could feel the blood draining back out of my head.

"The guys in the locker room are right. I am one lucky asshole . . ."

I laughed at his romantic side today as I sat up so that I could get a good look at his face. "I think my asshole would argue that it is the lucky one."

"Speaking of your asshole . . ."

CHAPTER TWELVE

"On your back, Loch," Marcus commanded. He had entered Master-mode, and there was no resistance from me that would have been tolerated. Of course, there was no resistance from me because I would have done anything for him without ever questioning it.

I followed my boyfriend's orders and lifted my legs as he pulled my ass to the edge of the mattress. Propping my feet on the top of his hairy chest, I watched as he lubed his big prick and then stuck two of those slickened fingers inside of me. He worked them around like the seasoned cocksman that he was. I was immediately ready for him to be inside of me.

Instead, he reached down to the carpeted floor and picked up the wrist restraints. Shaking them at me with a smirk on his face, he commanded me without even speaking. I put my wrists together and raised them in the air towards him.

Marcus' smirk changed to a smile as he strapped the restraints into place and made sure they were secure. He was quite pleased with himself, and I was quite pleased with him, as well.

"Lift your arms over your head," he ordered. His voice was so husky with desire that he practically growled.

I lifted my arms, wondering what he had planned, but knowing that whatever it was I would be safe and I would enjoy it immensely.

Marcus smiled at me like a jackal, lowered his head, and rubbed the top of his head up my stomach and chest. His short cut hair was sharp and tickled my skin as he moved up my body. I squirmed back to get away from him, but he was careful to hold me down. When he got to the top of my chest, he rubbed the top of his head against the underside of my arms, making me explode in a fit of laughter.

Lowering his head, Marcus pushed his noggin through my up-stretched arms until my wrists were resting on the back of his thick neck. He was now on all fours above me.

"Put your legs on my hips, Loch," Marcus commanded.

I did as I was told and saw exactly what he was doing. Placing my shins on the channels that ran from Marcus' crotch to the top of his hips, I held onto his sides to hold myself off of the mattress. Marcus held us firmly in place with one muscled arm while he scooped his other arm under me, supporting me.

Marcus Battle was so strong that he could easily support both of us in this awkward position. I used his support to hook my long legs together over his backside. I was now hanging underneath him as he was crawling on the bed.

We stopped in the middle of the bed, where Marcus reached down with one hand and fed his big horse cock into my tight hole. I moaned as my anal ring stretched around his mighty girth and was pushed all the way down his long shaft. Marcus filled me up, but not completely as I swung beneath him.

Marcus was on the same page as me, like usual, so he swung his hips forward, moving me off his dick, and then swung me back, fully impaling me on him. He continued to keep me swinging as we both groaned with pleasure.

"Now, are you able to think straight enough to begin our negotiations, Loch?" Marcus asked as he looked down at me. He hit my ass with his crotch and sent me swinging again.

"Really?" I asked in disbelief, my mouth completely dry.

"My cock gives you clarity, doesn't it?" he asked, completely serious. He moved his hips forward and caused me to swing away from him again.

"Yes, Master."

I watched as his features darkened and his eyes narrowed. Marcus wanted to fuck me hard and fast just as much as I wanted him to, but Marcus was patient and truly did know what I needed. He had the will power to deny himself the opportunity to give it to me. And that was just one of the things that made him such a special NOMAR.

I watched as he swallowed hard and redirected me. "I said earlier that I would like to wake up each morning with your lips around my cock."

"Yes, and I agreed to that."

"Now, what would you like in return, Loch?" Marcus continued to swing me back and forth, driving his big dick inside of me over and over.

"I would like you . . . to give me one . . . hard fuck each . . . night before going . . . to sleep. It can be quick or slow, but it has to be hard," I told him, pausing each time that his long rod delved deep into my ass, punching my prostate along the way.

"Just one?" He smirked.

"You know me, Master. I will lie under you the whole night, every night, while you rail me out, but I think we have to have limits."

"Yes, we do," he agreed. "I will agree to that."

"Thanks. Your turn."

He swung me forward again and commented, "We're being so formal."

I laughed. "There is nothing formal about this negotiation."

"No, I guess there's not. I would like you to entertain my friends."

"I would be glad to do that for you, Master, but I have some stipulations."

"Yes?"

"I always want you there, of course. And I don't think we should do that very often. We barely have time for ourselves, unless you want to spend less time with me," I said, realizing with a rush of emotion that, for the first time, maybe our goals were not in sync.

"Never, Loch, never."

"That's good. So, do you mind me asking why you want to share me?" I asked bluntly.

"I don't want it to appear that we are a sole unit — better than everyone else."

"I don't want that either, Master."

His smirk was back on his face. "Then I will agree to fuck around with you and some friends on occasion, but not often."

"You honor me, sir," I said jokingly.

"I think it is the other way around, but we have beaten that horse to death. It is your turn, Loch." Marcus gave me another hip check just to drive his words home.

"Fuck," I groaned.

"You like that, Loch?"

"Yes, sir."

He growled, "Then tell me your next demand so that I can continue."

"I know that I can't be with you on game days, but could we still be together without anybody else on Sundays?" I felt my face flush with heat even as I asked it.

Marcus raised an eyebrow.

"I don't want our new roommates to . . . interfere with our time together on those days."

"Maybe you could . . . give them something on game day and then they could leave us alone on Sunday," Marcus suggested.

"That might work, but you wouldn't be able to

participate," I said quickly.

"I'll be working out, anyway."

"So will I, apparently."

"Agreed," Marcus chuckled. He swung me forward again, slamming me back onto his rock-hard cock on the swing back. It felt like he had a baseball bat between his legs and he was swinging for the fences.

"Anything else, Master?" I asked, hoping to speed up this negotiation so we could get back to screwing. I could tell from his hesitancy and his face that there was something else which I guessed he was having trouble saying.

Finally he said, "My Dad and brother are coming to visit this year. To watch me play."

"Cool. So are mine, I think." I loved the idea of meeting Marcus' family and dreaded the idea of him meeting mine.

"I would like you to . . . show them a good time."

"Okay," I said, without giving it too much thought. I would do anything Marcus asked me to do, so this wasn't that awful in my book.

"It will keep them relaxed for the games and keep you out of trouble while I am away," he said, informing me of his thought process. I could see that he was struggling with this decision.

"I am at the Battle Family's service."

"Really, you don't mind?" he asked with disbelief.

I rolled my eyes at him and said, "Don't you know by now that I would do anything for you?"

"I do know that, but is it fair for me to ask this?"

"It is something a Master would ask of his Servant, and you are definitely my Master."

"Don't think that I'm going to ignore the fact that you just rolled your eyes at me."

"Sorry, Master."

Marcus swung me three times, each time slamming himself

into me deeper and harder than the last. That let me know how pleased he was with me, like I didn't know already.

"You are truly amazing, Loch."

I don't know about amazing, but I am horny as hell!

My cock was so hard that it was threatening to burst. "Are we finished yet? Because I don't think I can take much more . . . negotiating," I told Marcus in exasperation.

"Patience, Loch, patience. You don't have any other stipulations?"

I thought for a second and then said, "I want to go away every once in a while and have a session of bondage like we enjoy."

"Done."

"And can we still have at least one surprise during-the-day fuck in public like we did last year?" For the last two years, Marcus would sometimes surprise me by appearing outside of one of my classes. We would sneak into the public restroom and bang or I would blow him somewhere semi-private. It had been a real thrill for both of us and something that I wanted to continue to do.

"I would like that," he said gruffly.

I guess that I was affecting him more than he was admitting, but he was being betrayed by his body. "Now, I'm finished," I said abruptly.

"Tell me what you want, Loch." Marcus' voice was deep and husky with lust.

"I want you to fuck me, Master."

"I thought I was doing that already." He smirked.

"Please, Master," I said, whining the words.

"Is it what you need, Loch?"

"It is what I need and want, Master, more than anything." My voice was now matching his in tone.

"Good."

Marcus didn't say anything else as he fucking pumped his hard cock into my swinging ass with such force and speed that we both came within minutes. It was one of the most explosive orgasms that I had ever experienced.

Chapter Thirteen

After a month of blissful, non-stop sex, classes started for the fall. Marcus and my new roommates spent most of every day at football practice and class, so I was on my own a lot. I tried not to be a bother, but usually I had already finished my homework by the time they got home and was ready to hang out.

We soon fell into a routine, and I was much more settled when I got comfortable with the bus routes near our house. Sometimes I waited on campus at the library for Vance, Jordan, Marcus, and Finn to finish practice and we rode home in a golf cart belonging to the football team. It was a happy time for me, and I felt settled and safe for the first time in years.

Marcus kept me filled with either his big cock or a load of his hot spunk so that I wouldn't miss him when we were apart. Our rules were working well, and we modified them on the fly if we needed to. All five of us became even closer friends, and I enjoyed hanging with the other three when Marcus needed to study or sleep.

The first home football game was approaching when I decided to talk to Marcus about our plans. It was Thursday night, and he was soaking in a hot bath after a long practice.

Slipping into our bathroom, I sat down on the flat top of the bathtub and said, "Hey."

He opened his eyes, saw me, and asked, "What's up?"

"Nothing," I answered, suddenly shy about how I was going to talk to him about this weekend.

"Something," he said. "You know you can't hide anything

from me, Loch."

"I know. I was just wondering about this weekend."

"Ah. The game and all that it entails," he said, his face visibly relaxing.

"Yes, sir."

He looked at me with such fondness in his eyes that I thought I could hear my heart beat faster. I had the strong urge to jump into the tub with him. A naked Marcus Battle was a thing of beauty and one that I usually could not resist for long.

Marcus said, "I think the boys are pulling for you tonight."

"Pulling for me?" I asked in confusion.

He chuckled and the humor in his eyes shone more brightly. "They decided to pull straws to see who would get to . . . entertain you on Friday."

"Oh, they did, did they?"

"Yeah." He chuckled.

"I'll just have to see about that," I promised. "Don't they have to abstain the day before the game like you?"

"Please!" he answered, rolling his eyes. "Those three don't have my . . . dedication."

"Or your willpower," I added.

"I don't have much willpower when it comes to you."

"Me either!" I chuckled. Absentmindedly running a fingertip across the tattoo of the Kenan Bell Tower on his side, I remembered when we got our complimentary tattoos. Marcus had just played in his first bowl game and we had gone out for the night to celebrate and wound up at a tattoo parlor. I got a beautiful rendition of the Old Well above my heart. The two tats were major symbols of the University of North Carolina, as well as being pretty obviously sexual.

Turning heavy-hearted suddenly, I asked, "Will you miss me?"

"Are you kidding, Loch? I already can't wait until the game

is over in order to see you again. You are my fucking drug and I can't seem to get enough of you."

Well said, Master. I felt a lot better instantly. "I will miss you as well."

"Good. Now, get lost."

I laughed as I stood up and left him in peace. Walking out to the living area of the house, I saw Vance, Jordan, and Finn watching TV.

"Fellas," I said as I took a seat on one of the arms of the couch.

"Loch. We thought you and Marcus had . . . retired for the night," Vance said.

"So did I, until I heard that we were going to pull for me," I said with a smirk.

"We?" Jordan asked, hitting the pause button on the remote.

Finn yelled, "Marcus can't keep his trap shut!" I was sure that it was for Marcus' benefit.

"Of course," I answered Jordan.

Vance asked, "What, you want to draw also?"

"Yes, Vance."

The three boys looked at each other in confusion. "Maybe he misunderstands what we are drawing for," Vance stated.

"I understand perfectly, Vance. We are getting ready to draw straws with the winner getting to spend Friday with me," I said with a smart-ass tone.

"So, I'm pretty sure he knows what it means," Jordan said sarcastically.

"How could you draw then, Loch?" Finn asked.

Now that I had their complete attention, I paused for dramatic effect. "I get to participate, and if I win, I get to not be bothered on Friday," I finally said, like even a child should have known that.

"No way," Jordan immediately said.

"Fuck, no," Finn chimed in.

Vance agreed. "I don't think so, Loch."

"Really? You know that I can put a stop to the whole thing with just a single word to Battle," I threatened with glee. I didn't want to spoil their fun, but I also liked the challenge of manipulating them, and I didn't want them to think of me as a done deal, either.

"You wouldn't!" Jordan hissed.

I put them out of their misery by agreeing with them. "You're right. I wouldn't do that to you guys, but I do want some skin in the game."

My three roommates looked at each other and seemed to agree. Finn spoke up, "But your pull is too punitive."

"Wow! Good word, Finn," I said with an incredulous look on my face that made Vance and Jordan laugh.

"You pre-law now, Finn?" Vance smirked.

"I agree, Counselor Finn. What if I change mine to be *if I win, I will get to choose who I spend Friday with?*" I asked.

A deep voice boomed at us from the hallway. "You should never negotiate with Loch, unless your cock is buried inside him at the time." We looked up in unison, and I saw a wet Marcus Battle standing in the doorway, wearing nothing but a towel slung low around his hips.

"Master," I mouthed in awe, making sure no sound escaped my lips. I did not want to announce that I considered Marcus my Master. That was a fact kept between my boyfriend and me.

"Now you tell us, Battle," Finn told him.

"He will manipulate the hell out of you guys," Marcus said, chuckling. "I'll take him out of your hair." He turned his laser-like gaze on me and his eyes were smoldering with heat. "Loch, get your ass in my bed."

I stood up and bolted to our bedroom without even thinking about it. Marcus' draw on me was so strong that I was almost unable to resist him.

"Stop," he demanded.

I stopped in my tracks at the doorway leading to our bedroom.

"Would you like to pull your straw before you go to bed, Loch?"

"Yes, sir," I answered, holding my breath hopefully.

"Damn!" Finn hissed. "Marcus completely can shut Loch down in a heartbeat."

Vance laughed hard and said, "Oh yeah, Loch is a huge ball-buster with everyone but Marcus."

Jordan agreed by saying, "Battle is Loch's fucking kryptonite."

"And the kryptonite says that you can pull your straw before submitting to me," Marcus said. His use of the word *submitting* practically had me wet and unable to speak.

"Thanks," I finally croaked out.

Vance went to the kitchen and returned with four straws and a pair of scissors. I watched as he lined them up and cut them into different lengths. He turned to my boyfriend and asked, "Battle, will you do the honors?"

"Sure," Marcus said, moving towards the coffee table.

"You want to get the longest straw," Vance said, making the rules official. He handed the four modified straws to Marcus. "Because in Loch's case, longer is better," he said with a snort that made everyone laugh.

Marcus turned his broad back on us and called out, "Loch, come here." I was still frozen in place where I was when he told me to stop.

"Don't give him an advantage, Battle," Finn whined.

I stood up and walked in front of my man. Marcus reached out to me while holding me in place with his eyes. He reached up with his right hand and gently touched my mark and then his thumb came to rest on my lips.

Immediately parting my lips, I let his thumb slip inside my mouth and begun to suck on it with passion. I watched as the thin line of his mouth suddenly turned into a huge smile.

"I can read your mind almost as easily as if it was my own," he said softly. When he spoke again, he used his Master voice, saying, "On your knees, Loch. I'm going to make sure that you don't cheat by giving you my straw to keep you busy. Get under that towel."

I dropped to my knees and was already pulling at the edge of his towel before he was even finished with his command. I could see that his big cock was making a substantial bulge in the cotton fabric, so I was more than anxious to get it into my hot mouth.

"God damn! Battle knows what to do with him," Finn pointed out in admiration.

"I should hope so. They've been together for three years," Vance pointed out.

My head was now under Marcus' towel, and my tongue had found the big apple-head of his cock. I licked the leaking pre-cum like it was a melting ice cream cone. A big hand on the back of my head urged me forward, so I unhinged my jaw and let him slide into me.

"Loch has simple needs," Marcus said in his deep voice. "He needs to be full of big thick cock meat regularly. And he needs to have boundaries set and followed. It's that simple. If you can do those two things, he will open to you like a beautiful flower."

I didn't know how to take Marcus' philosophizing about me, so I continued to thrust my mouth back and forth along his thick shaft while I listened.

"He's a fucking cock hound," Finn said.

I felt Marcus sharply turn his head towards Finn. "We don't treat him like that, Finn," he said sharply. Turning back to me, Marcus put a hand on the towel where I was bobbing my head up and down on his pipe. "It doesn't make him less of a person or a man. It doesn't make us better than him. It's not a cut on Loch—it's just what he needs. And what he gives in return is the most valuable and special gift of all."

My heart swelled with pride for Marcus Battle. He had always been my biggest defender, and I loved him for it. I sucked with gusto, making long pulls that hollowed out my cheeks with the effort.

Marcus used the top of my head for what I assumed was to line up the straws in his hand. He had the perfect big mitt for this game, because his hand was large enough to hold all of the straws firmly and yet cover up their length.

"Who wants to pull first?" Marcus finally asked his boys. The mood in the room had suddenly gone very quiet, but now my roommates whooped and hollered as they stood up to grab their fate. "Keep it covered until everyone has theirs and then we will reveal all at once."

Judging by the commotion around me, all three guys had picked and then Marcus said to me, "Loch, lift your hand up." I did and he placed a straw in my hand. I could tell right away that I wasn't the winner, but it was hard to be sad about that when Marcus' cock was firmly planted in my throat and mouth.

"Everyone ready?" Marcus asked. His voice had gotten a lot huskier and his throbbing cock told me that he was close to his climax. I was amazed that he could still exhibit such control of his body even when he was on the verge of exploding.

Everyone said that they were ready, except me. I was still holding my closed hand up away from the towel. Marcus counted, "Three, two—"

Suddenly it occurred to me that he was planning to come at the same exact moment that we were going to reveal our straws. He held my head locked in place with his hand as his big cockhead bullied its way into my tight throat.

" — One, reveal," his voice boomed.

I opened my hand just as a torrent of hot musky nut juice shot down my throat. Marcus' small whimpers of release went unheard as Vance, Jordan, and Finn all yelled and excitedly compared their pieces. Someone picked my piece off of my open hand just as Marcus released my head and pulled back out of my throat. My mouth flooded with his salty spunk, so I swallowed and resumed pumping his hard dick for more.

"Finn is the winner," Marcus announced.

"I don't think he is the only winner," Vance said.

Jordan laughed and asked, "Did you just blow a load down Loch's throat, Battle?"

Finn chuckled and said, "I've never heard him so quiet."

"He has simple needs," was all Marcus said.

CHAPTER FOURTEEN

I skipped my Friday morning class in order to soak in our bathtub with the water as hot as I could stand it. Marcus had made sure that he gave me a fucking for the record books the night before. Of course, it was impossible for me to ever forget Marcus Battle, so it was unnecessary, but it was a nice way to start the weekend without him. I knew that it was his way to say that he would miss me, and I couldn't fall for him any harder.

I was still soaking when Finn knocked on the door. "Loch, you in there?"

"Don't be shy now, Finn," I said, raising my voice.

He opened the door, cautiously looking around. "You've been in here a while."

"Should I be somewhere else, Finn?" I was beginning to enjoy making the oversized footballer squirm.

He shifted uncomfortably from foot to foot and I could see that his cock was starting to harden inside his silky basketball shorts. "I . . . I . . . just thought . . ."

"You thought we would already be fucking by now, Finn?"

"Yeah, kinda," he finally admitted with a sly smile.

"Let me finish up in here, and I'll be with you shortly. Is that okay?"

"Yeah. It's all good with me." Finn's voice had already dropped an octave with lust and desire. He was more than ready to go. I watched as he left the bathroom, closing the door behind him.

Letting the water drain out of the tub, I got out, dried off, and took care of some grooming issues. My mind wandered to what Marcus was probably doing. I figured he was probably working out or watching game video and I took a few seconds to contemplate the likelihood of whether he was thinking of me or not.

Deciding not to even bother getting dressed, I walked completely naked into the front of the house. I could hear the sounds of someone lifting weights, so I headed to the dining room, which we had converted to a weight room.

Finn was lying on his back on top of the weight bench and Jordan stood over him spotting. I watched them for a few seconds. They were focused on the weight bar and seemed to be totally unaware of me.

When Finn finally let the weight bar come to a rest and blew out a deep breath, I decided to act. "Finn, I'm ready to fuck now," I said as matter-of-factly as I could.

Both boys sharply looked up at me. "Jesus, Loch!" Jordan mumbled. Finn didn't say anything, but his gaze hungrily roamed over my naked body.

"Too much?" I asked with a raised eyebrow at Marcus' roommate who had also become mine.

Just looking at Finn's face, I knew that he didn't think it was too much. I slowly turned and headed up the stairs, aware that both of their gazes were still on me. Marching myself right into Finn's bedroom, I took a deep breath of the masculine aroma that permeated the room.

Opening the blinds and letting some light into the room, I turned around and saw Finn in the doorway. He was wearing a ripped tank top with spaghetti-thin straps over his broad shoulders. The sides were ripped almost all the way down, giving me a good look at his smooth muscled chest and hinted at his amazing abs.

Finn was a redhead who had no body hair whatsoever, except on his ass. He kept his body shaved clean at all times, which had prompted me to ask him the first time that he, Marcus, and I had fucked around this summer why his ass was hairy. He had answered that he wasn't able to see it or it would be shaven also. Finn had tried to use some depilatory cream on it once, but it had just made his asshole burn.

Unlike most redheads, Finn's skin was beautifully tanned, probably from hours spent on the football practice field. His nipples hung from his pecs like grapes waiting to be fed into Dionysius' mouth, and I licked my lips in anticipation. He had an average length cock that got fatter as you approached the head, which was small. The whole visual effect was of a bottle of soda tapering to the bottle cap.

He was sweating, which explained why he grabbed his tank top, pulled it off, and said, "I need to shower."

"Do you?" I asked lustfully.

His eyes widened. "You don't care?"

"I prefer you don't."

"You a freak, Loch?"

I chuckled. "Probably. I just know what I like."

"And what is that?" Finn asked.

"All things men," I answered easily.

"What's that mean?"

I stepped towards him and said, "I love everything about men — their looks, their bodies, their voices, their muscles, their cocks . . ." When I got to this last one, I had reached Finn and jerked his shorts off. Grabbing his wrist, I pulled him into the bedroom and closed the door behind him. "I love the way men smell, the way they sweat, the things they say, and the way they move."

Knowing the effect that my words were having on him, I was able to easily push Finn down onto his bed and kneel in front of him. He probably assumed that I was going to blow him, but instead I picked up his foot and unlaced his sneakers. I soon had him completely naked.

"Loch?" Finn asked so quietly that it sounded like a moan. I sat back on my heels and looked up at him. "Yes, Finn?"

He blurted out, "Will you let me command you?"

"Let you?"

"Yeah."

"Finn, it's been my experience that you either command or you don't. You shouldn't have to ask for it, and I certainly shouldn't have to grant you permission."

"I know, but you seem to respond so . . ." I didn't interrupt him, but waited for Finn to compose his thoughts. "So compliantly when Battle commands you." His tanned face flushed dark pink.

"You want me to be compliant?"

"No, that's not really the word that describes it . . ."

Suddenly seeing the path he was trying to go down, I raised an eyebrow and asked, "You were turned on when I was subservient to Marcus?"

"Yes." He exhaled sharply.

"And you see yourself as the one in control?'

"Yes." His thick cock jerked as the spongy shaft filled completely with blood.

I nodded my head. "Then why didn't you just take control once you came in?"

"You have such a connection with Marcus that I didn't think you could respond the same way with me unless you—"

"Unless I pretended to," I finished for him.

"Yes."

"Well, you are probably right about that. I'm not one for pretending, but I definitely will give you a shot at being a commanding presence in our day together. I promise to not try to manipulate you . . . too much."

"Thanks, Loch. I know that I really shouldn't ask for anything else since you are already giving me this gift, but I can't help myself."

"No problem," I answered, reminding myself to wait and be directed. It was not my natural state, but my summer work with Mr. Lewellyn and my bondage work with Marcus had taught me well.

Finn looked at me and I bowed my head, waiting for his command.

"Would you shave my ass, Loch?"

"I would, sir." I did not move.

"Okay." He exhaled. "Can we do that now?"

"We can, sir." Once again, I made no move to stand.

Finn stood, and in my mind, I could see the look of confusion on his face as he looked down at me. "Oh," he suddenly said, like the light bulb had turned on above his head. "Into the bathroom, Loch."

I looked up, stood, and went into the bathroom. Finn followed me in and got out some shaving cream and a disposable razor. "Can I use this?" he asked.

"Yes, sir."

Finn handed both objects to me. He watched me standing there holding them for a few seconds before he said, "You sit down on the edge of the tub, and I will lean over the counter." He assumed the position.

Running my hand lightly over the skin of his ass cheek, I could feel the small sharp hairs that were growing out from his pores. "Would you like me to shave your whole ass, sir?" A real Servant would never ask this question, since he would wait to be directed or he wouldn't do it. But I was not his Servant, and there was no danger of me being punished and I didn't want to screw up his ass, so I asked.

"Yes," Finn said, his voice husky with desire.

I decided to forgo the shaving cream, using my hand and my tongue to find the hairs that needed cut. Finn shivered each time my sandy tongue ran across his smooth ass cheeks.

If I found a hair, I ran the razor over it with nothing but my saliva as surfactant.

Reaching between his outstretched legs, I wrapped my hand around his fat cock, finding it to be hard as an iron girder. Finn was obviously turned on by what I was doing to him. I continued to shave and lick him even as I stroked his huge dong.

When Finn's ass cheeks were smooth as a baby's bottom, I moved onto his crack. I needed both hands for that—one to hold open his ass cheeks and the other to carefully shave the small hairs away. It was slow and dangerous work, but I was careful and thorough.

"Loch." Finn moaned as my tongue got closer and closer to his asshole.

"Would you like me to stop, sir?"

"Hell, no!"

I slowly and carefully finished, brushing the quarterback's asshole with my fingertips as I did. Finn shivered and his whole body shimmied. Before I could even sit back, Finn spun around and stuck his flaming hot cock inside my open mouth. He pumped his hips forward two or three times before he lost his shit and blew a big load of hot cum into my mouth. I was so surprised by the quick face-fuck that Finn's spunk poured into my mouth, making me gag with the force of it.

"That was fantastic, Loch. I can see why Battle is so enamored with you," Finn told me as he pulled his dick out of my mouth.

I sat back on the side of the tub and tried to wipe cum off of my face. I couldn't help myself from asking, "You think he is enamored with me?"

"Please! That boy will cry when you get called to Service."

The thought of Marcus caring about me that much filled my heart with pride, but the thought of him being wrecked and me being without him was too painful for me to think about for long.

"I probably won't get called . . . I have missed my window."

"Your window?"

"I'm too old, Finn. Nobody wants a Servant as old as me."

"Fuck! If I go pro, I would take you in a heartbeat," Finn said, his voice seething with desire.

"Thanks, Finn. You ready to fuck?" I didn't want to think about this anymore, and nothing changed the subject for a NOMAR like the thought of fucking.

"Always," he hissed, releasing his breath.

I bowed my head and waited for his command.

"On the bed, Loch." I stood and followed him into the bedroom where I mounted the footballer's bed.

"How would you like me, Finn?"

"I would like you multiple times, Loch," he said in a smoldering tone as he jacked his fat tool.

I responded by raising my legs and putting my ankles on Finn's thick shoulders. "You better get started then." I smirked.

"Don't you worry," Finn said with a grin as he plunged his fat cock into my exposed hole.

He was no Marcus Battle, but getting plowed by Finn definitely kept my mind off of missing my football-playing boyfriend, and for that I was grateful.

CHAPTER FIFTEEN

I attended the football game with my old friends from my freshman dorm. Marcus had a hell of a game, scoring two touchdowns and earning more than one hundred total yards in the air and on the ground. I yelled so loudly for him that I was hoarse afterwards and a little drunk when I said goodbye to my friends and made my way down to the tunnel leading to the locker room.

The security guards there knew me, but still made me wait against the wall. I was drunk enough not to care about a little rest against a cool cement wall, but I didn't feel like I was slurring my words or swaying at all, and I didn't feel sick.

I finally took a seat on the ground to wait. Marcus must have been doing a lot of press interviews, because it took forever for him to come out of the tunnel. Most of the hangers-on were gone by then, and I had contented myself with making mental patterns out of the cracks in the cement.

I felt him before I was even aware that he was there. Suddenly alarm bells rang in my head and all the hair on my arms stood at attention. I looked up and I saw Marcus towering over me.

"Marcus," I said, my voice so breathy that it sounded like the wind rushing through the tunnel.

Marcus raised one eyebrow, studied me for a moment, and then extended his hand to help me up. He didn't say my name or anything else.

I took his hand, feeling the immediate sexual electricity between our skins. He easily pulled me to my feet and I lunged at him, enveloping him in a hug.

"You played a fucking amazing game, Marcus!" I said a little too loudly.

"Thank you." Marcus smirked. "Loch, you seem to have had an especially good time during the game . . ."

Oh, shit! Now, I was in trouble.

I reverted to Servant-mode instantly. "Yes, sir."

"In the car, Loch." Marcus' voice was positively icy.

I opened my mouth to apologize or explain—I wasn't really sure which when I saw his eyebrow lower and his smirking lips become a thin line. "Not a word," Marcus growled.

The threat of what might happen to me if I talked was just as delicious as the thought of what Marcus was going to do to me for getting drunk. I felt my dick harden in my shorts.

Closing my mouth, I turned on heel and headed up the ramp. I could hear Marcus behind me, and he kept a safe distance between us—one that kept my senses and cock on high alert, but that was just far enough away that it caused me pain. I knew that he was doing it on purpose, and I was helpless to do anything about it.

Marcus and I marched out of the stadium to his truck. Once inside the cab, he didn't start the engine right away, instead gripping the nape of my neck with a strong hand. I looked into his eyes, and my breath caught in my throat. He was my Master, and I was undone under the gaze of those eyes. His face softened.

"You enjoyed the game, Loch?" he finally asked.

"Very much, sir. You were like a giant amongst men, Master."

"Were you turned on watching me?"

"Yes, Master."

"Show me," he commanded as he unzipped the fly of his shorts and slid to the middle of the bench seat.

I couldn't help but smile as I slithered off of the seat and onto my knees. Reaching into Marcus' fly, I wrapped my fingers around his ever-hard joint and weaved it through the fabric to the light of day.

"Master," I sighed as I impaled my mouth on his long thick cock. He tasted fresh like soap and he started leaking his sweet nectar as soon as I touched the sensitive skin of his glans with my lips and tongue. I licked it like a soft-serve ice cream cone—worshipping it, worshipping him. Taking him almost all the way into my throat, I sucked him with long pulls that gave him the maximum contact of my mouth on his skin.

Marcus was soon at the edge of his climax, and it made me wonder how long he had been in this horny state. He normally would not let me suck him if he was displeased, so I knew he was hurting for release and I dedicated myself to giving him the best blowjob ever.

"Loch," he said softly as he wove his big fingers into my short hair. He fell over the edge and exploded in my mouth. The force of his ejaculation was so powerful that I thought I might have damaged my throat for a second as cum poured out between my lips and his shaft like a water balloon that had just burst.

Swallowing to keep from choking on the hot salty deluge, I savored the taste and heat from my Master. It was my favorite thing in the whole world to have a belly full of his spunk right before he filled my ass with his big cock and another load of hot cum.

I worked to clean his cock. I didn't want to miss one single drop of his delicious goo. I searched his shaft for cum that had blasted out of my mouth during his climax.

Marcus worked to grab my hair and he used it to tilt my face up to his. "Loch," he called softly. My gaze found his and I melted into it.

I let his cock pop out of my mouth but kept his giant cock-head resting on my lips and said, "Master."

He smiled and closed his eyes, like my use of that title did things to him that I couldn't see. He moved his hand down to my cheek and he rubbed it with an over-sized thumb. "I can tell that you enjoyed the game. Thank you for showing me."

I smiled as I darted my tongue out to the base of his shaft and found a glob of cooling cum. Retracting my tongue quickly, I swallowed it down, making sure he saw.

His breath caught in his throat and his eyes blazed at me. "You know that I have to punish you, right?"

"Yes, sir."

"You know why, don't you?"

"Yes, sir," I answered even as I explored the rest of his shaft with my tongue, my eyes never leaving his.

"I don't mind if you drink, Loch, but you cannot drink like that in public."

"Yes, Master."

"Tell me you know why," he commanded.

"It is for my protection, Master."

"Yes." Marcus continued to stroke my cheek. "You have to be on high alert at all times. I have always loved that about you, and until today, I have always been impressed by your . . . diligence. Something bad could have happened to you."

"I'm sorry that I disappointed you, Master," I said with sincerity as I removed my lips and tongue from my biggest distraction. "I guess that I just felt safe, since I was with my friends and meeting you afterwards."

"You will not do it again," he said firmly. His voice was so husky and deep that I could feel it reverberating in my throbbing dick.

"No, sir," I said, swallowing hard.

"Good." He studied me attentively, his whole palm flat on my cheek now. "You may get drunk with me, Loch. I have always got your back. You know that. I will always protect you."

"I do know that, Master." His words made my heart swell, as well as my already hard cock.

"Let's go home so I can start punishing you," he said matter-of-factly as he helped me up onto the seat.

"Yes, sir!" I said enthusiastically.

Marcus drove us home. The house was empty, because the boys were out celebrating their victory on Franklin Street. As soon as the door was locked behind us, Marcus pointed with a big arm to our bedroom.

I was more than willing and practically ran to our big bed. Marcus followed me like a silent shadow, looming large and mysterious behind me. He closed and locked our door. Surprising me, he went to our closet and retrieved some of our bondage supplies. We didn't usually use them at home, instead saving them for special occasions when no one was around but us.

Marcus saw the questioning look on my face when he turned around. He was holding a blindfold, a gag, and multiple restraining straps. "You know that I must punish you, Loch."

"Punish or reward, Master?" I asked flippantly.

"For you, they are basically the same thing," Marcus said with a smirk.

Tilting my head to the side, I made the facial expression that told him that I couldn't argue with that logic.

Marcus crawled onto the bed and began to strap the blindfold onto my face. He knew that this truly was a punishment for me, because I enjoyed nothing more than watching my big man as he penetrated and destroyed my puckered hole.

"I want you quiet," Marcus commanded me as he placed the rubber bit of the gag into my mouth and strapped it into place on the back of my head. He rolled me over onto my stomach and stretched my arms out in front of me. Bending my arms at the elbows, he connected my wrists and strapped a Velcro restraint onto them. My Master placed a pillow on top of my bound arms, so that my head could rest comfortably on it.

My cock was so painfully hard that I needed my release already. Knowing that the delay of my climax was just as much punishment as any of the rest of this, I conceded that it was going to be a very long time before I got any relief.

Marcus strapped Velcro bands around my biceps. These had silken cords attached to them and when he bent my knee and pushed me into a kneeling position with my head on the pillow, I knew that he was going to attach the other ends of the cords to my thighs. That way I would be unable to move from this kneeling position.

"I want you open to me at all times," he told me, before he went to the closet and returned with a spreader bar that he had used to hold my legs apart.

There was nothing in the whole world that I wanted more than that. As humiliating and helpless as it was to be in this position, I would stay in it for the rest of my life if it meant that I had Marcus' attention.

Marcus moved off the bed and opened the nightstand drawer. "I want you wet for me," my boyfriend said as he poured lube into my enflamed hole and then followed it with two thick fingers.

I howled in pain behind the gag as his thick digits stretched my anal ring open. Marcus worked those fingers in and out of me like they were a shorter, thinner version of his manhood. The pain soon turned to sheer pleasure. He played my asshole like a freaking virtuoso, and I was putty in his hands as he did it.

The removal of Marcus' fingers left me feeling empty, but I knew that it signaled that he was ready to fuck me, so I could do nothing but smile to myself around the gag. I was so ready for this that the punishment was almost worth the crime.

"I want you full of me," Marcus grunted as he pushed his giant cock head against my puckered hole and penetrated me further than anyone ever had before. His wide cock split my anal ring so far open that I thought he might have torn it, but I was soon squeezing his mighty shaft with it as he slid down inside of me without too much pain so I knew I was okay.

When Marcus hit the bottom of my ass and held us in place, he had completely penetrated me, and I was truly full of him like he had said he wanted me to be. It was a wonderful feeling, and I felt lightheaded from it. I could feel his thick cock thrumming inside of me like a second heartbeat and I used my ass muscles to try to milk his long shaft as he held it thrust to the maximum depth inside me.

Marcus knew this position was a punishment for me, because besides watching him destroy me, I loved to touch as much of his body as possible when he was fucking me. Now, I could do neither.

My boyfriend leaned forward over my back, suddenly pinched my nipples hard, and said, "You feel so fucking good, Loch. You make me want to punish you every day."

I was just letting my mind wander to that place. A place where I was bound and restrained every day with Marcus fucking filling my ass up to the brim—when he pulled back and then slammed his fat cock back inside of me.

"You are mine," Marcus yelled behind clenched teeth.

Yes, I am.

Another deep, hard thrust. "You will follow my orders where your safety is concerned."

Yes, I will.

Marcus slammed into me with such force that it threatened to knock me over onto my side. "I know what is best for you, Loch, and I will do what I need to do to protect you."

Yes, you do and will.

This time Marcus plowed into me and continued to pound

my poor hole. "Fuck! This sweet ass is made for my cock. It belongs to me."

Yes, it was and yes, it does.

Marcus Battle said nothing more. There was nothing else to say. He had made his point and now punctuated it by fucking my asshole like it needed to be fucked.

CHAPTER SIXTEEN

M arcus fucked me once more in this bound position. I heard him go to the bathroom and clean up. Then I heard him put his clothes on. He sat down on the bed near my head.

He unstrapped the rubber gag from my head and said, "I don't want to hear a sound out of you. Do you understand, Loch?"

I nodded my head by way of answering.

"Good." He held something hard up to my mouth and I recognized it as the top of a bottle of water. "Drink," he commanded.

I drank, heard him screw the top back on the bottle, and then he opened the bedroom door. Marcus carefully closed the bedroom door behind him, and I recognized this as another part of my punishment.

Being with Marcus was like a drug for me, and if I was unable to be with him, then I was in the pain of withdrawal. I knew that he knew there was nowhere else I would want to be except with him, so he was using this to punish me further.

I lay against the pillow and fought against the urge to feel sorry for myself. Marcus was gone for a long time, and I finally fell asleep in my restraints.

Hearing the bedroom door open, I woke with a start. The door closed and locked before Marcus sat down on the bed near my head. I knew it was him because I could feel the electrical charge between us and I could smell him.

Marcus stroked my back as he sat beside me. "Loch," he

said softly.

I didn't respond.

He held the water bottle back up to my lips. "You make me very proud of you, Loch." I drank the water greedily. "You take your punishment like a man, and that pleases me very much."

Taking the water bottle away, he started to unhook some of the straps and said, "I think it is time we get you into a new position." Marcus was becoming quite adept at the bondage game and he soon had me on my back, legs spread wide open, and in the air.

"There. That's better, huh?" He fed me a little more water which almost choked me, before chasing it with his hot dick.

I sucked my big boyfriend with all of my might, showing him how sorry I was and how important he was to me. I slobbered all over his big knob and soon all I could taste was his delectable pre-cum.

Marcus didn't say a word as he pulled his cock out of my hungry mouth, climbed between my legs, and drilled it into my tight poop chute. My back arched and I held my breath as he plunged all the way to the bottom of my deep mine shaft.

"Jesus! You feel so fucking good. Each time, your sweet ass squeezes my cock like it has never met it before," Marcus grunted as he repositioned himself for a better angle.

I wanted to tell him the same thing, but didn't want to break his rule about not talking. I would just have to tell him with my ass.

My football-playing boyfriend fucked me hard and fast — drilling into me like he was going to strike oil. Instead he filled my empty mine shaft with his hot sticky cum and then proceeded to fuck me again without even pulling out.

It was an amazing display of power and stamina. I felt so fortunate to have found Marcus and even more lucky that I got to be with him. After coming for the fourth time since we came home, he pulled out of my ass and let my mouth clean him up before he gave me the rest of the bottle of water.

"Thank you, Loch," he said softly as his thumb stroked my cheek. "You make me very happy."

I was so in love with this man that I wasn't able to think of anything else except pleasing him. He was everything to me—my world, my life, my hopes and dreams.

Marcus got dressed again, and when he opened the bedroom door this time, I heard the TV playing a football game and voices. I guessed that the boys were probably home from Franklin Street and my heart hurt as I realized that they were going to have some fun without me tonight. I hated missing out on anything.

"Battle! We missed you. Why didn't you and Loch come uptown with us?" It was Jordan's voice right outside the bedroom door.

"Something came up," Marcus said firmly.

"Where's Loch?"

"He will not be joining us tonight."

"For real?"

"Yes. He is being punished."

"Fuck me," Jordan said, stretching out the words. "What did he do?"

"That is for Loch to contemplate. Now, let's go watch the game."

"Cool. We brought you guys some food."

Their voices faded as they left the hallway. My stomach growled at the mention of food. I was happy that Marcus had not immediately told the boys what I had done, although I really wasn't that ashamed of it. It was more something between my Master and myself, and that was how he was keeping it.

The next that Marcus came into the bedroom, he had something with him that smelled like food. My mouth started to water and my stomach growled at the smell.

"Let's get some food into your system, Loch. You can't live solely on my spunk."

I opened my mouth in anticipation, but instead Marcus began to unstrap my restraints. He repositioned me so that I was sitting upright on the bed but still spread-eagled. My arms were clasped in the small of my back, and my wrists were bound together again. An image of my G.I. Joe doll from childhood flitted across my mind. This position was the only way that I could get Joe to sit up on my bed.

Marcus sat down on the bed between my spread legs with his hands on my hips. He lifted my hips and I smiled as I realized that he had swapped out the silken cords for some bungee cords that allowed for some movement.

I felt his hairy legs slide underneath my ass and then I was suddenly sitting on his crotch. Marcus' big body was now pressed up against mine, and I could feel the heat from his cock searing the sensitive skin of my ass.

Some of his cum was starting to drip out of my ass, so Marcus played the little Dutch boy and put a plug in my ass. Unfortunately for him, his cock was not a very good plug for my leaking ass, because it took up so much room inside me that it actually forced more cum to flow out of me to make room.

"There. That feels good doesn't it?"

I nodded in agreement.

"Open," he commanded.

I opened my mouth, and he inserted something hot and small. I closed my mouth, chewed, and savored the unmistakable taste of a pizza roll. I swallowed it down and he inserted another one.

Marcus' cock was throbbing inside of me as he patiently fed me. He took turns to let me sip sweet tea through a straw after every two bites.

"And now for something healthy," he said as he inserted

something larger into my mouth.

At first it was good — ranch dressing. But then I tasted cauliflower, which was a taste that I hated. I scrunched up my face, but kept chewing.

"Don't disappoint me again, Loch," Marcus growled. His voice was dripping with passion and authority.

I swallowed and opened my mouth for more. This time it was broccoli with some ranch dressing, which I considered to be even more disgusting than the cauliflower. But I chewed it like it was birthday cake and managed to swallow it.

He followed the veggies with more tea and then wiped my mouth. "I know how much you like your desserts, Loch, so I've brought you something very special."

I heard a spoon clink against glass and then enter my mouth. I used my tongue to scrape the food off of the spoon and tasted banana pudding. It was my favorite dessert. I made a low moaning sound from deep inside my chest as I savored it.

Marcus began to laugh and couldn't seem to stop. I felt his fingers on my head, and then suddenly the blindfold was removed from my eyes. I blinked in the low light and saw that it was night already. There was one nightstand lamp on. I blinked at Marcus, seeing him in all of his naked glory so close to me.

"How much do you love me right now?" he asked as he scooped another spoonful of pudding into my mouth. "My Loch loves a big cock in his ass and a mouthful of cream, does he not?"

I laughed as I chewed and swallowed the bite. Some pudding had stuck to my lower lip, and Marcus used his thumb to wipe it off and then he inserted it into my mouth. My gaze locked onto his, and I sucked his thumb with all the passion and energy that I would have sucked his cock.

But something was different. I felt the change in his

electrical field before he probably even realized it. His gaze penetrated right into my soul, and both of our breaths became shallow. Marcus put the bowl of banana pudding down and pulled his thumb out of my mouth. It was wet, and he kept it at the corner of my mouth as he gripped my head with the rest of his hand. His right hand soon joined his left, holding my head between them.

Marcus traced my lips and then he tightened his grip on my head. He was so close to me that I was frozen in place, mesmerized by his slightest little movements.

I felt like something was happening between us. Something that was different than anything that had happened before. Every little bump and vein on the surface of his cock tickled my ass as he throbbed inside of me. His masculine, musky smell was in my nose. My eyes were full of him and my skin goose-pimpled at his touch. This had to be what it felt like for a Servant to be with the person who was their true Master.

With a sharp intake of breath, Marcus pulled my head the last few inches towards his and ever so softly our lips touched. I didn't think it was really happening at first, because kissing was something that we had never even come close to before. His kiss was so light that I could barely feel it, and then he pulled away from me. Our lips stuck slightly together as he pulled his head back and that was the only way that I was sure that the kiss had actually happened.

I said, almost as a sigh, "Mast—"

Marcus quickly pulled my lips back to his, effectively silencing me. This time he crushed my lips with his kiss and I followed his lead, eagerly eating his face. I loved how the long hairs of his beard and mustache tickled every part of my face that touched him. There was no tongue from Marcus and I certainly was not going to jinx this moment, so I kept mine in my mouth as well.

Slowly, I began to pump up and down on my man's hard

pole while we were still locked in a lip-lock. I could feel Marcus' hands on my hips, ever so slightly pulling and pushing me up and down his hard shaft. My hands were still bound behind my back, but I fantasized that I was running them all over his beautifully sculpted physique.

I was suddenly alive with energy and sensation. Everything felt better—Marcus' big dick felt thicker and more defined, his cockhead seemed to be punching further into me than ever before, his smell was more intense and powerful, his eyes brighter and more soulful, and the taste of his skin was sweeter than ever.

Almost without me even realizing that I was close, my body pushed me over the edge of my climax. My back arched, my lips broke free from his, and my face pointed straight up as the piss slit on my cockhead opened and I spewed a volcanic amount of man-lava between our sweaty chests. My cock pumped its release just as my ass muscles constricted and clamped down on Marcus Battle's magnificent rod.

"Fuck!" he groaned. "That's the shit right there." He grabbed a handful of my hair and pulled my face back down to his. His beautiful golden eyes were so alive with light that it looked like a video of a hot sandstorm—swirling, mesmerizing, and dangerous.

He kissed me harder and fucked me the same way at the same time. My ass muscles were all that I could focus on, because I was overwhelmed by every neuron in my body firing at the same time. I bore down on him, squeezing him harder and tighter than ever.

Marcus groaned into my mouth as he reached his relief and exploded inside of me, dumping another load of hot cum into my already overflowing ass.

The load that poured out of my man's fuck stick was neverending. He had already come so many times today, and to think that he could produce this size load was unbelievable.

Marcus Battle was a man of simple pleasures, but one thing was for sure—his balls held a deep well of his seed, and he was determined to plant every single one of them inside of me.

CHAPTER SEVENTEEN

Marcus kept me bound in our bed in various positions throughout the night. We fucked so many times that I lost track, and in the morning when he released me, I could barely walk. I spent Sunday soaking in one tub of hot water after another while Marcus constantly checked on me.

My overwrought boyfriend was afraid that he might have broken me, but I reassured him constantly that I would have not changed a thing. We had turned a new corner in our relationship, and there was absolutely no way I was going to retreat now.

By Sunday afternoon, I was feeling much better and finally emerged from the bedroom. Jordan, Vance, and Finn were all hanging out in the TV room watching the NFL.

"Well, fuck me! Look who it is," Finn said when he saw me.

"What the fuck did you do, Loch?" Jordan asked with a shit-eating grin spreading over his face.

"We are not going to discuss it," Marcus' deep voice boomed out from behind me. "Loch has served his time, and we will now move on."

"Served his time?" Vance asked. "Is that why he is walking so gingerly, Battle?"

"Some punishments are better than others, Vance," I said with an exaggerated wink.

"Wanna sit over here, Loch?" Jordan asked as he swung his legs off of the couch.

"No, thanks. I'll just stand over here. You guys played a helluva game yesterday," I told them as I high-fived my three roommates while I crossed the room.

We spent the rest of the day watching football and discussing their game from the day before. We went out to eat bar-b-que for dinner, and our weekend soon came to a close.

The following week was a busy one for all of us. Besides classes, I had a big meeting with my academic advisor on Wednesday. Marcus and the boys were leaving for an away game on Friday to Boston and wouldn't be home until Sunday night. I had planned on writing a research paper and doing laundry for the house since I would be alone.

Wednesday after classes I stayed on campus. Hanging out in Davis Library, I waited until five minutes before my appointment with my advisor before heading out.

Professor George's office was on the second floor of the psych building and smelled like old books and stale cigarettes. He was a physically repulsive man who combed long wispy strands of hair over his bald dome in the semblance of having hair. He was nice enough, but talked down to me through most of the review of my courses.

"So, you seem to be well on your way to graduating. You have taken or are taking exactly what you should be in order to get a well-rounded base in psychology."

"Thank you."

He looked up from my paperwork and studied my face for an instant. "What are you planning on taking next semester and next year?"

"I will take Behavioral Psych II and Abnormal Psych II next semester and next year I would like to apply for the Honors Independent Study."

"Really?" he asked in disbelief. His eyes went right to my mark.

"Yes, really," I said sarcastically.

That seemed to snap Professor George out of his head as

he looked down at my grades. "You have much higher marks than I first assumed, Loch."

I didn't say anything, but let him see my displeasure with the straight line that my mouth made.

"And you still let the football team fuck you?" he bluntly asked out of nowhere.

"One of them," I threw back at him. "Even though it is none of your business."

"You are right," he immediately said as he rose to his feet and came towards me. He put a hand on my shoulder and gave me a squeeze. "I didn't mean to offend. I was just curious."

"Well, you offended," I said curtly.

"Perhaps I can make it up to you," he offered. I wasn't looking up at him but I noted the definite change in his voice—it was suddenly much huskier and that spelled danger for me.

I shot out of the chair before he could react. Standing now, I saw that he was between me and the door. He put his hand on the bookcase across from him, blocking my exit.

"What's the hurry? We are just talking."

"I am leaving," I said firmly.

"Now, now, I could make it difficult for you to get the classes you need next semester if you are not nice to me," he said creepily.

"This is over. It's not happening," I said with as much confidence as I could muster. I stepped towards his arm, and he lunged at me. His hand was on my ass before I even realized that he was actually going to try to manhandle me.

I was both taller and wider than the professor and, thanks to the three years of weightlifting that Marcus had insisted that I do, I was stronger than the creep. Taking a fast breath, I cracked him in the side of the face with my elbow and then kicked down on his shin. I heard the bone break before he wailed out of pain and collapsed at my feet.

Standing over Professor George, I said, "I will be filing a report with the dean as soon as I leave here." With that, I turned and walked out of his office. True to my word, I filed a sexual harassment complaint with the University on my way home.

They had already heard from the psych building and the professor was on his way to the hospital with a broken leg. I was worried that it was my word against his, but knew that I had done the right thing regardless of what happened.

I decided on my walk to my car not to say anything to Marcus. He was already so vigilant about my security that he was liable to not let me out of the house for the next month. If it ever came up, I would just pretend that it had slipped my mind because of his away game. I didn't like not being truthful with Marcus, but at the same time I didn't think anything good could come from telling him either.

I got my paper finished and went to sleep early. I was just eating some cereal on Saturday morning when I got a text from Marcus.

Hey, you up?
Yes, I am, smartass. Aren't you getting ready for the game?
I am. Just checking up on you.
Thanks!
Did you see that crazy vine about one of your psych professors?
What? *Oh shit.*
There's a video about one of your profs being carried out in a stretcher.
Oh yeah? *Now what do I do?*
Wait . . . didn't you have your meeting with your advisor?
I did.
There was no response—not even a bubble on my *iPhone* that Marcus was composing something.

My phone suddenly began to play *Uptown Funk*, which was my ringtone for Marcus Battle. I almost dropped it into my cereal bowl, I was so surprised.

"Hello?"

"Loch." Marcus' voice did not sound pleased, even though he had just said one word.

"Hey, Marcus."

"Was that professor your advisor, Loch?" My boyfriend's tone let me know that he was not open to joking or elaboration. Marcus wanted the facts and he was not playing around.

"Yes, sir." I wasn't sure why I reverted to his title, but I felt like I was in trouble and that might get me some kind of reprieve.

"What did he do, Loch?" Marcus had switched to Mastermode and there was almost nothing I could do to disobey him.

However, I didn't want him doing anything to get into trouble, so I lied. "Nothing."

"Loch, don't lie to me. He did something. Now, tell me what he did."

I swallowed hard, sat up on the couch a little straighter, and informed him, "He tried to force himself on me."

There was silence on the line at first and then I heard a low rumbling growl like a bear coming out of its den. "What did he do, Loch?"

"It was really nothing. He pawed at me and I handled it."

"I will kill him," he growled.

"No, Marcus. I punished him." I wanted to plead with Marcus to not make a big deal out of this, but he was a smart guy and would come to that conclusion once he had time to think about it.

"You broke his leg?" Marcus asked softly.

"I did."

Marcus chuckled on the other end of the line.

"I released my inner Master and channeled you, sir," I said with a giggle.

"I'm proud of you, Loch, and it will set a good precedent for people not to fuck with you."

"Thank you, sir."

"But you know that I'm angry with you for not telling me right away, don't you?"

"I figured you might be, Master, but I handled it, I filed a report with the University, and my heart was in the right place. Besides, I didn't want to take your focus away from the game."

"Why do you say that?"

"I was afraid of your reaction, Master."

"You did nothing wrong, Loch, so why would I be angry with you."

"Not me, Master."

"Oh," he said. "It probably is a good thing that I am many states away from him."

"The University will take care of him. You should concentrate on your game today."

"You are an amazing man, Loch, but you know that I will not allow anyone to hurt you."

"Yes, I know, and I am thankful, but in this case I took care of it," I said firmly.

"I'm willing to concede that."

"But what I want you to do, Master, is to take the anger out on your opponents today. I want to see you cracking heads and know that is what you are doing. Can you do that for me?"

"I can and will," he finally said into the phone.

"Make me proud, Battle," I said to end my pep talk.

"See you soon, Loch. Stay in the house with the doors locked until I get home."

I rolled my eyes and said, "Okay, right."

Marcus played an amazing game. He didn't score a touchdown, but he did have more than a few pivotal blocks that had the announcers comparing him to Heath Miller of the Pittsburgh Steelers with his multi-faceted game. Carolina won the game and continued our hot streak.

I was really proud of Marcus and rewarded him with twenty-four hours of pleasure upon his return. He didn't have to strap me down to punish me this time, but he did anyway. He told me that he had considered my reasons for not telling him the story immediately and took that into review when deciding on the punishment.

Marcus had finally revealed that my punishment would be to have to wait one hour before he would touch me. It was a cruel punishment, because by the time he got home on Sunday night, I was completely horny for him. He elaborately told me that because my intentions were good that day that he would allow Jordan, Vance, and Finn the first hour to keep my mind occupied during my punishment. The boys had constantly been ribbing me once they heard what I had done to my Advisor.

I was strapped into place on the bed in the shape of a suckling pig on a platter on a dining room table. I was kneeling on the edge of the bed and leaning over my legs with my head up and my mouth open.

My roommates were extremely happy that Marcus was granting them the chance to fuck me after their long trip away. They cautiously asked me if it was okay with me to proceed and I assured them that Marcus and I were on the same page at all times. Jordan, Vance, and Finn took turns fucking my ass and mouth until each of them had dropped two loads of steaming man-spunk into me.

And the big man hadn't even gotten started yet!

CHAPTER EIGHTEEN

Summer quickly changed into autumn and each week pretty much followed the same pattern—classes, hanging out with my friends, football practice, football games on Saturdays and all-day fuck sessions with Marcus on Sundays.

I was in heaven of course, but my grades were slipping and I knew I was going to have to have a conversation with Marcus about cutting back. It really wasn't either of our faults, because we were drawn to each other more than ever. I found it incredibly difficult to keep my hands off him at almost all times and his lips found mine even when we were not fucking around. I couldn't bring myself to do it now, because it was homecoming week. Marcus' family was coming to town, and he had a huge game against ACC powerhouse Florida State which was going to be on ESPN for a national audience.

Putting my thoughts on the back burner, I made sure that my boyfriend had no drama to distract him from the game that week. His brother and father were due in on Thursday for dinner. Finn was going to stay at a fellow player's apartment so we were going to give his room to Mr. Battle. Monty, Marcus' younger brother, would sleep with him in our bed. That just left me without a bed, which was quickly rectified when Vance volunteered to have me sleep with him.

Marcus and I burned off the energy of waiting for his family by washing both of our cars in the driveway. It was a really nice day, and soon our shirts were off while we worked. It was almost the stereotypical wet hunk dream of all marked men, but a Chevy Tahoe pulled into the drive before I could live out all of the fantasy.

I could see through the windshield that an older guy was driving and a younger guy was riding shotgun wearing a set of white headphones. The driver got out immediately and rushed over to hug Marcus in a big bear hug. He looked just like his son, but only older and thinner. His big square jaw jutted out from a smooth-shaven face.

"Dad!" Marcus said, excitement coloring his tone.

"You look good, son," Mr. Battle said, his voice returning Marcus' excitement.

"Dad, you're early. This is Loch," the younger Battle said to the older one.

I stepped forward and extended my hand saying, "It's a pleasure to finally meet you, Mr. Battle."

He shook my hand and looked me up and down. "So, you are the man that my Marcus gives so much credit to for his play?"

I chuckled as I released his hand. "He does, but I still don't know why."

"Monty, get out here!" Mr. Battle yelled into the SUV.

Monty was already opening the door and I took him in as he walked towards Marcus to hug him. Monty was a high school senior who was the shortest member of his family, but he had a great barrel chest. He wore baggy shorts and a tight-fitting tank top that showed off his thick arms and chest. But his most amazing feature was a huge neck supporting a big head.

His blond hair was shaved close to his skull, and he wore a white baseball hat turned backwards. Monty had Marcus' amazing eyes — deep pools of swirling golden sand that seemed to be able to take in everything.

"Bro," he said as he gave Marcus a man-hug.

"You look good, Monty. No game this week?"

"No, man, it's a bye week." I knew that Monty played on

his high school football team and was a hot prospect among the college recruiters.

"Monty, this is Loch," Marcus said, introducing me.

Marcus' little brother turned his full gaze on me and suddenly I felt like a turkey on Thanksgiving morning. He actually licked his lips right before he said, "What's up, dude."

"Nice to meet you, Monty. I heard you verbally committed to Ohio State. Congratulations."

"Thanks man. It's going to be sweet."

I looked him up and down and asked, "Guard?"

An impressed look appeared on his face and he said, "Wow, Marc, a hot piece of ass and a sports guy. What more could you want?"

"Monty!" Marcus snapped. "You know I will not tolerate that."

"What?" Monty quickly asked, but he was unable to look at me.

"No problem," I said quickly, trying to cover the awkwardness.

"Let's go inside and I'll show you the house," Marcus said, changing the subject.

"I'll finish up here, Marcus," I said, indicating the hose and the still-soapy car and truck.

"Thanks, Loch."

After rinsing the cars off, I turned the water off, put away the rags and buckets, and entered the house. I found the Battle family in the weight room, where Monty was challenging his brother to see who could lift the most. They were pretty evenly matched, but Marcus' muscles were more developed, so they eventually won out.

I leaned in the doorway and watched my man as every muscle in his body flexed and tightened as he lifted. I could feel my dick getting hard and shifted it in my shorts before going to the TV room and flipping on Sports Center.

They eventually made their way out to me. Looking up, I asked, "Who won?"

Monty answered sullenly, "Marcus always wins."

"Looks like you might catch him soon though, Monty," I said encouragingly.

"Loch is probably right," Marcus admitted. "Once you get in that OSU weight room next year, you're going to be a beast."

"That's the plan," Mr. Battle said, affectionately hitting his youngest on the shoulder.

"Why don't you guys go get cleaned up, and then we can go get some bar-b-que," Marcus said to his family.

"Sounds good," Mr. Battle said. "Monty, bring our bags in."

Soon, Marcus and I were alone. "I'm going to let you go to dinner with them without me," I told him.

"Why?"

"They don't seem too comfortable with me around yet."

"They will be," Marcus said with a confidence that I wasn't sure he really felt.

"I'm not sure."

"Loch, I need to ask you something."

The tenderness in his tone really caught my attention, so I muted the TV and turned to face him.

"I don't think my dad and brother will ever understand you and me . . ."

"You may be right."

Marcus' face was neutral, but I could feel the conflict within him like a disturbance in the electrical field between us. "The only way that I can think of for them to understand what you mean to me is to have you show them."

"What do you mean?"

"I mean that I think you should show them." His tone was matter-of-fact, but his eyes were pleading with me. "Show them what you mean to me, Loch."

I realized what he meant and asked, "And you think that will work, Marcus?"

"I do. They could never question us again afterwards."

"Would you command me to do it?" I challenged him.

Marcus lowered his head and looked at me through his brow. "I would never do that."

"I know and I appreciate that about you more than you will ever know."

"I just think it would help . . ."

"I will be honored to show them then."

"You are the best, Loch!" Marcus stood up and approached me. He grabbed my face on each side and said, "You truly are the most amazing man that I have ever met." Then he crushed my lips to his in a hard kiss before separating.

"And I am yours," I said definitively.

"That's why I am the luckiest man alive. I'll tell them while we are at dinner." His smile lit up his handsome face.

"You are mine," I said softly.

"I am yours," he assured me just as his family members rejoined us in the TV room.

They left shortly thereafter and I went to dinner with some of my friends from the dorm. When I returned home, Jordan and Vance were home as well as all the Battle family.

"Loch!" Jordan yelled when he saw me come through the door. My NOMAR roommates always made me feel welcome.

I sat down to a vicious game of *Call of Duty* between Marcus, Monty, and Vance. Monty was victorious and received high-fives all around. Marcus' talk with his father and brother about me must have gone well, because when I slapped Monty's hand, he smiled at me and lustfully growled. Mr. Battle seemed to be even more uncomfortable around me, which I took as a sign of his acquiescence of the situation.

"Loch, can I have a word with you outside?" Marcus deep voice rumbled.

"Oh shit, you're in trouble now," Jordan chided me.

"If I was in trouble, Jordan, he would have told me to go to the bedroom, not outside," I said as I headed to the front door. I wondered immediately if it was off-color to say that in front of Marcus' family, but it was something I would normally have said anyway, so I was okay with it. Marcus had not commanded me to watch my language or not be myself in front of them, so I felt like he would not be upset with me.

As soon as we were outside, I asked, "How did it go?"

"Well. What NOMAR doesn't like to hear that they are going to basically get a Servant for the day?"

I chuckled and said, "Exactly."

"Monty is so full of seed he is about to explode, but my dad is more guarded. I don't know how he feels about you yet."

"I think he sees me as a distraction," I admitted with a sigh.

"Probably," Marcus agreed. There was silence as I looked up at the stars and he watched my face. "Do you mind doing this?"

"No. I would do anything for us."

"I know you would. I don't want my family to get in the way of us."

"What if your father asks me to stand down?"

"Stand down?" Marcus asked, seemingly confused.

"I can see him demanding that I leave you alone."

I saw the realization of what I was theorizing cross Marcus' face. "He might. He has mentioned it to me before that while he thinks you are an incredible gift to me, he also thinks that I probably should let you go, to be able to concentrate more on football and my future."

"Do you think that is true?" I held my breath after I blurted out the question.

"No. I have told you before that I think you are the reason

that I am as good as I am now. You saw this in me years ago and have produced it out of that lump of freshmen flesh like Botticelli sculpting David out of a hunk of marble."

"You give me too much credit."

Marcus' golden eyes picked up the lights from inside the house and shone at me as we stood on the darkened porch. "You enhance my game, my world, my life. I crack skulls on that field because I want to make you proud. I score touchdowns just so I can see your face afterwards and know that I have done well. And above all, I want to make you proud to be with me."

"I feel the same way about you, Master," I said as my voice cracked with passion.

"When I'm buried deep inside you, I want to know that I deserve to be there and that you are happy to have me there." His voice had suddenly gotten much deeper and lusty.

"Trust me, I am always happy to have you buried to the balls inside of me," I snorted.

Marcus reached out with a big hand and cradled my face with it. His thick thumb brushed my cheek. "Loch."

"Master," I said back heavily.

"You are mine."

"I am yours."

"And I am yours."

"Yes, you are."

"And nobody will come between us?"

"Nobody," I agreed firmly.

He smiled and said, "Then that will make me very happy."

"You know what will make me very happy, Master?" I asked coyly.

"I wish," he said with a laugh, already knowing exactly what I had in mind. "You've got to entertain Vance tonight and then my dad and brother tomorrow, so I think we are out of the question."

"I could blow you right now," I suggested. "It will help settle you for the game . . ."

"Well, if you think it will help," he said with humor as he pulled his basketball shorts down and revealed his huge one-eyed monster.

"It always helps both of us," I said as I dropped to my knees.

Chapter Nineteen

Vance had mostly let me get some rest when I spent the night in his room. He fucked me once before we went to sleep and then I blew him in the morning when we woke up. He had told me that he felt super guilty fucking around with me when Marcus was in the house, but it didn't stop him from busting his nut twice inside of me.

I showered and joined everybody sitting around the kitchen table.

"Marcus is gone to work out and watch game film," Mr. Battle said to me almost immediately when he saw me walk into the kitchen.

"I figured," I said back to him. "It's his usual routine." The more I could make it sound like Marcus was doing what he was supposed to the better, I thought.

"We won't see him again until the game," Jordan told the Battles.

"Where does he sleep?" Monty asked.

"At the football center," I answered. "He says that he can get in all of his workouts, attend class, watch film, and get his head on straight for the game if he immerses himself in it."

Monty looked at his father and said, "Damn! Am I gonna have to do that, Dad?"

"If you wanna be good," Mr. Battle said, without even thinking about it. I could already tell that Monty did not have the focus that Marcus did, and while he probably was very physically gifted, he was never going to be the student of the game like his older brother.

"So, what is the plan for today?" Mr. Battle asked the crowd, although he seemed to be focused on me.

"I have two classes this morning, and then I can meet you guys for lunch if you like."

"Jordan and I have class and then we have to join Marcus at the stadium," Vance said, dropping his dirty cereal bowl in the sink. He and Jordan both left as I wished them luck for the game tomorrow.

"We can hang out here and wait for you," Marcus' father told me.

"Cool. I'll go to class and then swing by here and pick you guys up and we will go to Franklin Street for lunch."

"You want me to give you something to think about during class?" Monty asked, his voice so full of lusty innuendo that I almost laughed out loud.

"You got something that you think might take my mind off of my studies, Monty?" I asked, joking with him.

"We can go back to the bedroom and I will show you," he promised.

I looked at the clock and said, "I've got time to blow you before I have to leave to go to class."

"Fuck me," Mr. Battle said in a whisper.

"Yes, let's do it!" Monty said, standing up and walking towards my bedroom.

"Mr. Battle, can I take care of your morning wood for you?" I asked awkwardly before leaving the room.

"Sure, if you don't mind," he answered awkwardly.

"Your son has asked me to take care of you and I would do anything for him, so let's go."

"Lucky son-of-a-bitch," Mr. Battle said to no one in particular.

Back in the bedroom, Monty already had his basketball shorts off when Mr. Battle and I walked in. His cock was at full mast, almost as long as his brother's but not nearly as thick. Monty had the same ridiculously large cock head on top of his shaft, just like Marcus. It was not proportional to his cock, so it made him look like he had a stick with a ball on the end of it between his legs.

I knelt on the heavy carpet in front of Marcus' little brother and wrapped my fingers around the base of his cock. It was already hot to the touch, leaking a drop of golden man-honey as I licked his big cock head.

"What are you doing in here?" Monty asked his dad.

"I got needs, too," Mr. Battle explained to his son. "I'm not dead yet." Marcus' father dropped his shorts and pulled a fat joint out of the fly of his boxers.

I inhaled Monty's cock as I moved my mouth down towards his short hairs.

"I don't think Loch wants to be sucking on an old man's donkey dick," Monty said. "Just sayin'."

"On the contrary, Monty," I said after I pulled his cock out of my mouth. Grabbing Mr. Battle's monster at the base, I pointed it at my open mouth. "This is the cock that spurted the seed that made my Marcus, so there is nothing more that I could want than to taste your father's magical elixir."

"Loch, you can call me Mike. If you are going to suck my cock, we should at least be less formal."

"Yes, sir," I said, before sucking his long thick cock into the back of my throat. Mike had the same cock that he had given his oldest son, except instead of having a huge cockhead, he had a small bottle cap.

I lapped up the pre-cum from Mike's drooling cock before moving over to his youngest son's and doing the same thing. Pulling on their balls, I sucked and licked the Battle relatives until they were on the verge of climaxing. Like most NOMARs, when they got to fuck around with a real live marked man, they were unsure what to do, so they reverted back to standing still and letting me do most of the work.

"I can't believe Marcus gets this any time he wants," Monty said in disbelief.

"It is amazing to think about," Mike agreed as I pulled on his balls while deep-throating his cock.

"I want this," Monty moaned.

Mike said, "Well, you know how to get it. Make the NFL, and you can call for a Servant with your signing bonus."

"But Marcus—"

"Marcus got incredibly lucky," Mike said, cutting his youngest son off in mid-whine. "You can't count on that." I looked up, and my boyfriend's father was looking down at me with such reverence that I couldn't begin to try to figure out what he was thinking.

An hour later I was sitting in class with a belly full of Battle cum. I had blown both boys and their father within the last twelve hours. Marcus had been right, because I felt closer to Monty and his dad now. But then Marcus was usually right with his decisions about me—he seemed to know me better than I knew myself, and he certainly knew what I always needed. Fortunately for me, he was committed to giving me what I needed at all times.

I didn't get much out of class that day because my head was full of visions of the Battle family gangbanging me as I lay bound on a big bed. I texted Marcus and told him that he was right about his family and then stared at the blank screen. I knew that he was too focused to even have his phone on him, but he would check it at some point during the day.

Finally class was over, so I headed back to the house ,where I picked up Monty and Mike. They were excited to get out of the house. I parked on one end of the main drag in Chapel Hill, and we were soon walking down Franklin Street, looking at all the stores, bars, and restaurants. Monty and Mike both bought Carolina baseball caps to wear to the game tomorrow and, with a lot of pride, I showed them Marcus' jersey for sale in the back of the Shrunken Head Boutique.

We ate at Blimpies and then had a quick beer at Four Corners just to say we did.

"What do you guys want to do now?" I asked.

"Fuck," Monty said, without any hesitation or shame at all.

"Monty!" his father snapped.

"Well, I do," he said by way of explanation while he looked at his father. "And Marcus told us we could."

Mike looked at me, and I said, "We better head back, then."

"Awesome!" Monty crowed. He practically ran back to the car.

I drove the short distance to the house in silence. The Battle boys weren't sure what they were supposed to say, so they kept quiet. I enjoyed the silence of the drive. The windows were down and the crisp autumn air was making my nipples hard as I drove towards two hard fuckings.

Once in the house, Mike told Monty that he could go first. It showed great restraint, and I suddenly saw where Marcus got his from. Monty didn't seem to have any of that restraint.

I followed Marcus' brother back to my bedroom and saw that he had already stripped before I could even close the door. His thick chest was absolutely smooth of hair and his cock was already hard.

"You want me to suck on you some, Monty?"

"No. I'm ready to go."

"Okay," I said, as I went to my nightstand and grabbed a tube of lube. Throwing it on the bed, I lay down flat in the middle and gave him a great view of my ass.

Pulling a pillow under my head, I listened as Monty jacked his cock with the lube. He clumsily crawled onto the bed on either side of my legs and then pushed his cock head into my crack. Monty missed my hole, but continued to try to push his dick into me.

I reached back and repositioned him onto my puckered hole. Immediately Monty pushed it inside of me. He was young and had none of the finesse or patience of his older brother, but his cock sank deep inside me to temporarily excuse those flaws.

"Damn, that's a nice hole," Monty commented more to himself than to me.

"You've got an equally nice cock," I groaned back to him.

Monty leaned over my prone body, held himself up by his arms, and fucked down into my tight hole. I knew that he was constantly watching his big joint disappearing inside of me and then suddenly reappearing with each thrust. NOMARs were prone to doing just that, especially if it was the first time that they had sex with a marked guy outside of a Service Station.

Marcus' little brother lost his shit quickly and pumped me full of his sticky semen. Rolling off of me and onto the bed beside me, he looked up at the ceiling of my bedroom and said, "Wow!"

"Did you like that, Monty?" I asked as I turned my head on the pillow towards him.

"Loved it. How many times does Marcus do that to you a day?"

"As many as he wants," I said with a grin.

"Fucking lucky as hell."

"We both are," I agreed.

"Although you feel so tight, that he probably doesn't take you up on your offers very often."

"You would be wrong to make that assumption," I said with a snort. "Your brother is the most sexual being that I have ever met . . . besides myself, of course."

"I could go again," Monty said, now that I had spurred his sexual competitiveness.

"Of course you can," I said as I reached down and jacked

his sloppy dick with my skillful fingers and palm until he was stiff as a board again.

"I want you up on all fours this time," Monty said. He was starting to get the hang of ordering me around.

I followed his command and was rewarded with a really hard and fast fuck from Monty, which reminded me of those I had received over the years from his brother. Finishing off our afternoon of sex, I rode Monty's long prong while bracing myself on his thick chest. He placed his thick arms behind his head and wore a huge fucking grin on his face.

"You enjoying the show, Monty?"

"Yes! You are amazing, dude."

"Thanks. I hope that you see me as an asset to your brother."

"Emphasis on the ass," he said with a chuckle.

I ignored him and climbed back onto my soapbox while I continued to slam my ass back down into his crotch repeatedly. "Marcus works very hard on the field, in the gym, in the classroom, and on top of everything he is super-nice and humble. I am here to reward him for all that more than anything."

"Rewarding me now," Monty groaned as he moved his hands to my hips and held me in place as he dumped another load of teenage cum into my sore hole.

I stayed quiet while he came back down from his high. Monty opened his eyes and looked at me curiously. "Would you come live with me next year, Loch?"

Totally shocked by his question, all I could muster to say was, "What?"

"Next year, when I'm at OSU, will you come and live with me?" The look on his face was completely serious.

"No, Monty. I belong to your brother."

"But I can give you all the cock that you need. I would keep you filled with my meat and cum around the clock."

I laughed at the thought of it. "I appreciate the offer, Monty, but there is nothing that would keep me from Marcus' side next year."

"What about the year after?" He was like a dog with a bone—stubborn as hell.

"I don't know what is going to happen, but I know that you would not want someone old and used like me. You will be at the start of your big-man-on-campus phase, and you will want to attract your own marked man to serve you." I had very little faith in that statement, but I said it with conviction anyway.

"You think?"

"I think your life is just beginning, and I hope that the same great things that are happening to Marcus happen to you as well."

"Thanks," he said, his pale cheeks flushed with color.

"I have to get a shower and try to win over your dad."

Monty's golden eyes twinkled. "Just do for him what you just did for me, and he will be eating out of your hand, bud."

"Oh, yeah?"

"Trust me," Monty said as he helped me lift off of him.

I didn't trust him, but I did agree with his assessment as to the best course to win his father over. Now, it was time to put the plan into operation.

CHAPTER TWENTY

Jordan, Vance, and Finn all came home after practice and were starving. Mike had brought a whole bunch of steaks with him from Ohio on ice, so he was busy in the back yard grilling. Monty was helping him with that, but was mostly gulping down beers and telling his dad about my ass, I was sure.

I had popped six potatoes into the oven for the last hour and was now making a big salad. I missed Marcus on nights like these, but I knew that he was doing what he had to do to stay focused on his dreams.

The conversation at dinner was mostly the boys telling Marcus' family stories about him and the team. We laughed a lot and ate even more. I tried not to overeat, because I was going to go work out shortly after dinner.

I was just wondering how Mr. Battle was going to manage the transition from the kitchen to the bedroom in front of all the guys, when Jordan stepped in and saved the day.

"Monty, you want to go with us to grab some killer ice cream?"

"Sure, man."

I couldn't help but notice that Monty was completely comfortable around the boys. He was used to being with football players, and he related easily to my roommates.

Jordan winked at me and said, "You want me to bring something back for you, Loch? Mr. Battle?"

"No thanks, Jordan," I answered and Mike echoed my words.

"I'll drive," Finn said. "You guys can jump in the back of the truck."

The boys flew out of the house, and suddenly the kitchen was very quiet. Just to cover the uncomfortable pause, I grabbed the bottles of salad dressings and headed to the fridge. Mike was behind me with the steak sauces and handed them to me as I held the door open.

Mr. Battle looked up from his hands and into my eyes. He cleared his throat and awkwardly said, "Monty says that I'm not going to believe the things that you can do."

"It's just fucking," I said flippantly, turning away from him to close the fridge door.

When I turned back around, Mike was still looking at me intently. He said, "It's something more than that. My Marcus has never gone against my advice before you came along."

I hadn't planned on going there, but now that my boyfriend's sire had brought it up, I was going to go there. I looked at him hard and asked, "And what was your advice to Marcus about me, Mike?"

"I told him not to fuck you." There was absolutely not a whiff of shame in him for admitting this to me. He was completely unapologetic.

I chuckled even though I didn't mean to. "When? When we first met?"

"Yes. I knew that if he fucked you, it would be harder for him to . . ."

I kept silent. My heart was overflowing with pride in Marcus for going against his father and following either his heart or his prick.

"Harder for him to break from you. Of course, I never dreamed that you would pick him. You had your choice of the biggest studs on the whole team, and you picked a scrawny freshman who didn't even come on to you."

"How do you know he didn't come onto me?"

"I know my son," he said firmly.

I chuckled. "We were both scrawny freshmen."

"Yes, and once you picked him, he was trapped."

Trapped? What the fuck was this man talking about?

Mike looked at me and his expression softened. "I didn't want to talk about this now."

"Wanna go fuck?" I asked him, cutting right to the quick of the matter.

"Yes," he said with a big sigh. "You're a good man, Loch. I can see that now." He was obviously relieved that I didn't make him say it.

Unbelievable. Accuse me of trapping your son and then have the nerve to still fuck around with me?

This was a new low for me, but I still held out hope that the whole process would be beneficial to my relationship with Marcus in the long run. I turned without a word and headed to his son's bedroom that he shared with me — the very cage of the trap.

Mike and I stripped off our clothes, and I sucked his long thick cock while he sat on the edge of the bed. I was delighted to see that he had a big furry chest covered in the same dark copper hair as my boyfriend. He was more physical this time, probably because we were alone and not in front of his youngest son. He played with my hair and stroked my shoulders while I blew him.

When he was hard, I pulled off him and lay down on my stomach. I lay face down and let him mount me from above. Mike's thick cock felt good stretching my sore hole further than it had been opened today and he soon sank all the way inside of me. I could feel his pubes tickling my ass cheeks as he hit the bottom of my ass.

"Fuck, that's nice," he growled above me.

"Better watch out, or you might get trapped," I said, just loudly enough for him to hear.

Mike froze in place, probably deciding what to do.

149

"You okay?" he asked, very much like something his oldest son would have done.

I made a humming sound since I wasn't quite in the mood to talk to him yet.

My boyfriend's dad pounded my pud for the next hour. He had the finesse and power that I had always admired in Marcus' fuckings, and he could fuck a lot longer without climaxing as often. There weren't many times when I was impressed with a NOMAR's skill set in this area, but this was one of them.

"You mind flipping onto your back, Loch?" Mike finally asked.

"No, sir." I followed his instructions, lifting my legs so that he could climb back into the saddle. Placing my feet flat on the top of his hairy chest, I bent my knees as he leaned forward.

Mike pointed his small cockhead at my asshole and sank his root back inside me to the short hairs. "Mind if we have a chat, Loch?"

I was taken aback at first, because I wasn't used to guys being able to delay their gratification once they had their cocks inside me. But he was Marcus' father, so I should have guessed. I nodded my head in consent.

"This is something special," Mike told me as he looked down at where his cock was pulling out of my ass. He slammed it back home again.

"Thanks."

"I can see why Marcus is unable to . . . separate from it."

It? Separate from it?

"How many of your roommates have gotten to hit this?"

I thought about not answering at first because it really was none of his business, but his tone suggested that it was small talk and I really didn't have anything to hide from him. "All of them."

"And you think that is helpful to Marcus to have to

constantly worry about who is fucking you?" His tone was not so casual now.

"It is only with Marcus' permission that I fuck other people. He recognizes what I need and takes care of me."

"I'm sure he does," Mike said. "I'm just saying that all of this drama has an effect on his focus."

"There is no drama," I reiterated.

Mike sighed. "Loch, I have advised Marcus to drop you. Not because you aren't good for him, but because I believe that you take his focus away from his real purpose. Nothing against you — it's not personal. I would advise him to drop anyone who would interfere with football."

"I don't feel I interfere with football, Mr. Battle."

He slammed into me again. "I know you don't, but I'm sure that you do. Hell, I can't think about anything else and I'm not even trying to play football."

"Marcus has told you that?" I challenged him.

"No," Mike immediately answered. He slammed back into me in the silence afterwards before saying, "But then he doesn't have to." He let out a big sigh before thrusting his hips forward a few times. "I can tell that you care for him, so I know that you will do the right thing."

"The right thing?"

"You need to leave Marcus. He can't leave you. He's a strong man, but nobody is that strong," he said with a laugh as he sunk back into me again. "Your ass is so fucking tight and sweet."

"I don't want to leave Marcus. I think we are good for each other," I said with confidence.

"I know he believes that also. He has told me that he gives you a lot of credit for bringing out the beast in him."

I nodded as I braced for the next thrust of his hips. This was not news to me, because Marcus had always given me the credit.

"You can take a year off," he said as he continued his fuck-ing. He talked through it, "You can go to him after he signs his NFL contract. I'll even pay for the plane ticket."

"It would be a year and a half, and I don't need your money."

There was no way in hell that I could go a year and a half without being with Marcus Battle.

"You'll consider it, because he is important to you," Mike said with confidence as he neared his release.

I kept quiet and held onto Mike's big shoulders as he fuck-ing tore me up. This was one of the hardest things that I had ever had to endure — getting lectured to by a man who was fucking me at the same time. Marcus' dad grunted through his climax as he continued to pound me into the mattress with great stamina. Mr. Battle wasn't able to sustain his pace, and he eventually hesitated and then fell apart.

Mike collapsed on top of me, held my shoulders, and spo-radically moved his big cock into me and back out again. His breathing soon returned to normal, but he didn't rise off of me.

"Loch, let me tell you a story," Mike said into my neck. "I've never told my boys this before."

Now he had my attention.

"When I was a senior in high school, I was a cocky eight-een-year-old who played three sports and was on top of the world. I got a scholarship to wrestle at the University of Iowa, major league baseball teams were scouting me, and Penn State wanted me to play football for them."

Okay. A little history lesson.

Mike continued, "One of my buddies had a little brother who was marked. At the beginning of my senior year his fa-ther approached me. He told me that he had asked his son who he was attracted to and the kid had said my name."

Oh fuck! I see where this is going . . .

"My buddy's dad asked me if I would take Kent under my

wing—basically giving me permission to fuck him." Mike got a little choked up here, but quickly recovered. "And fuck him I did. Kent had a nice tight ass like yours, Loch, and I did my best to keep it punched open every day. I taught him how to suck my dick the way I wanted it done, how to take a hard deep fucking, and how to serve me in every way sexually that I could think of."

Now, Mr. Battle lifted himself up onto his arms and looked at me.

"By the end of my senior year, I couldn't live without Kent. It was the greatest year of my life and when he asked me not to go away the next fall, I knew that I couldn't leave him, so I said no to all of those teams and all of those schools. I stayed home in that little town in Ohio and do you know what happened?"

I hesitated trying to decide if I should say it or not. Finally, the quiet and the heartbreak was too much for me to endure so I blurted it out, "Kent left to go to The Service?"

"Yes," he said, nodding. "He went to the SA and never came back."

"You feel cheated."

"Yes."

"And you don't want that to happen to Marcus," I said distantly. Suddenly, it was all fitting into place.

"Yes."

"It won't," I said firmly.

Mike stared into my eyes. "You say that now, but the lure of having him close will be too much for you."

"You don't know me as well as you think you do, Mike," I challenged him. I knew that he was right about one thing— the thought of being separated from Marcus would be a searing pain that I didn't think I could live through, but where he was wrong was thinking that I could experience that pain earlier than I needed to.

I'm not that strong.

"So, you will let him go?"

"When it's necessary, but that decision will be made by your son and myself together. We are a team, Mike."

"That I am sure of, Loch," he said as he rose off of me and pulled his long dick out of my sore hole. "If I've learned anything this week, it's that the two of you are on the same page."

"You got that right," I said with a chuckle.

"Thanks for this, Loch and I hope that you will consider what I've asked you."

I didn't answer, instead just said, "I will always do what is best for Marcus, and he will always do what is best for me." Heading to the bathroom, I felt empowered by the way that I was firm with Marcus' dad, but knew that this wasn't over.

CHAPTER TWENTY-ONE

I went to the game the next day with Monty and Mike, but the air was frosty between us. Monty drew so much attention to the fact that he was with a marked guy that I had to tell him to knock it off. Mike was just worried about the game.

Marcus played really well, scoring twice on receptions, but the Heels lost the game by two touchdowns. The Battle family seemed happy with my boyfriend's play, so maybe I wouldn't be blamed for the loss—at least not this week.

After the game, an usher of some sort came to escort Mike and Monty to the locker room. I told them that I would meet them in the tunnel later and they happily left me behind. Walking down to the tunnel, I was starting to feel sorry for myself, but my body was ringing like a bell because I was about to see Marcus for the first time in two days.

I waited in the tunnel, chatting with some of the security guards about the game. I got the familiar tingling in my balls that Marcus was nearby, so I looked up and was surprised to see that he was alone. He stepped over the barrier with his long legs and stared me down.

"Loch," he growled from deep inside his chest.

"Marcus," I growled back.

He put a big hand on my shoulder and turned me towards the top of the tunnel. His hand moved down to the small of my back, signaling me to start walking. My skin was on fire at his touch and my cock immediately swelled with blood.

"Are we not waiting for your father and brother, Master?" I didn't consciously use that title. It just seemed to flow out of my mouth when we were fucking or when both of us were completely tuned into each other like now.

"Not today, Loch, not today," he answered me in his usual cadence.

"You played a great fucking game today, Master."

"Thank you, Loch." We were almost to his truck.

"Every time I looked up you were in the end zone," I said with a snort.

Marcus looked at me with such desire burning in his golden eyes that my breath caught in my throat. "I'm getting ready to be in your end zone, and something tells me that I'm going to score often and easily there today also."

"Yes, sir," I said, completely breathy.

"Now, don't speak again until I tell you to." His command of me was so firm without the slightest bit of superiority or degradation to it. It wasn't that he was my better — it was just what needed to be done and both of us knew it.

We rode in silence during the short trip to our house. Marcus put his hand on the inside of my thigh and held me in place until we arrived. Once the truck came to a stop, we both bolted for the door. Stripping our clothes off as we ran to the bedroom, we were soon in each other's arms with our mouths on each other.

Marcus soon pushed my shoulders down and I lowered to a kneeling position. I immediately took his giant lap-hog into my mouth and tasted his delicious skin. The electrical charge that flowed from his prick to my lips and tongue was incredible, but it was the clear golden honey that slowly dripped out of his cum vent that I was really after.

I sucked him in long drawing pulls that hollowed out my cheeks as I tried again and again to impale myself fully on Marcus' fuck stick. His breathing became shallow and his legs started to shake slightly as he neared his release.

I pulled on his big balls, trying to milk them of the

delectable spunk that they held. Marcus held my head in place as his back arched, his piss hole opened, and his nuts sent a tremendous volley of hot salty cum racing up his shaft. He spurted strand after strand of thick man-goo into the back of my throat as I swallowed it down as fast as he could produce it.

"Oh, fuck, I've missed your sweet mouth. It belongs on my cock."

I wanted to confirm that for him, but he had not given me permission to speak yet, so I contented myself with lapping up the excess cum that was clinging to his wet shaft.

Marcus finally pulled me to my feet, hugged me tightly, and then laid me on my back onto the bed. it wasn't what I wanted, and he knew immediately.

"Not what you want, Loch?" he asked with a raised eyebrow. He wasn't used to me interrupting him in the middle of a good fuck.

I didn't answer, since I wasn't sure if I was allowed to or not. instead I stood up from the bed, spun Marcus around, and pushed him onto his back onto the mattress. Grabbing the bottle of lube from the nightstand, I slicked up his meat beast and then climbed onto the bed. I straddled him while his hands help guide me down onto his pike.

Marcus filled me up like no one ever had. As his bolt slid into place in my lock, I felt safe and completely at ease, as I always have with his weapon completely buried inside my ass. I squeezed his hard shaft as it pulsed and throbbed deep inside me.

"Now, Loch," Marcus' deep bass voice rumbled.

I wasn't sure what he meant, so I tried to twist my face to see his, but he stopped me. Marcus put one arm around my waist and the other hand on the middle of my chest. His big feet snaked their way around my legs at the ankles. He held me down and in place.

"Tell me what is wrong, Loch, now."

"Master, all is right with the world now that I am here." I was still debating whether to burden Marcus with my trivial worries.

"Loch, I am connected to you. And in more ways than just my cock inside that sweet ass of yours. If you are feeling even the slightest off-center, I can tell. Can you not feel the same thing from me?"

"I can, Master," I said, knowing completely what he was talking about. My dick hardened to a painful erection.

"Then tell me now, Loch."

His constant use of my name had quite the effect on me or maybe it was the enormously thick piece of man-meat that was throbbing away inside of me, but either way I felt light-headed. "I did what you suggested, Master, and let your brother and father see what I had to offer."

"Yes, they told me in the locker room." There was not even a whiff of judgment in his voice.

"Your plan to have them see what I bring to the table worked, Master. But it might have worked too well."

"My father liked you too much?"

"Yes, sir." I wanted to tell him the things that Mike had said to me, but suddenly I found myself very emotional. It was a strange feeling — to be on the verge of tears, have a raging erection, and have a huge hard cock planted firmly inside of my ass. I had never experienced anything like it before.

Without me even saying anything else, Marcus raised the hand that was holding my chest up to my face. He gently glided his long rough finger under my eye and scooped up the tear that was resting there. I had no idea how he knew it was there and was once again in awe of him.

I managed to choke out part of what was on my mind, "Master, you know I would never want to interfere with your — "

"Loch," Marcus said firmly, interrupting me.

"Master," I answered.

"Do you trust me?" My boyfriend repeated his finger swipe of my other eye, finding another stationary tear. This time he brought his finger to his face and I knew without even looking that he had put his finger in his mouth.

"Implicitly, Master." It thrilled me beyond belief that Marcus had grown so much in our three years together. He was almost fully invested in us now.

"You have always been what I needed. You have done nothing but enhance me since the day I met you. You saw my potential and have done everything you could to bring it out in me."

Marcus had told me this before, but never with so much feeling. I had believed it each time, but never felt it until now.

"Are you mine?" he asked, his voice suddenly changed from soft and warm to hard and commanding.

"Yes, sir."

"Do you belong to me?"

"Yes, sir."

"And if I give you a command, then you will be compelled to follow it?"

"Yes, Master."

"Then I command you to be at my side until graduation day, Loch. Tell me that you understand me."

"I understand, Master."

"Show me that you will comply with my command, Loch." His voice was in complete Master-mode.

I reached down and stroked my painfully-hard cock. It only took a few movements before my back was arching and my nuts exploded in an amazing white arching rainbow of spunk.

"There it is," Marcus growled as my ass muscles constricted even tighter around his shaft. "You are mine."

159

"I am yours."

"You are not going anywhere, Loch."

"Not without you, Master."

"That's what I'm talking about!" Marcus said excitedly as he lifted my hips and fucking tore me up from below. He fucked me so hard and fast that I could feel that he was at peace with me, our relationship, and his decision.

CHAPTER TWENTY-TWO

The rest of the football season was inconsistent for the team, but very consistent for Marcus and me. The team won and lost some, but made it to a bowl game in Florida the week after Christmas. I made plans to visit my family for the holiday and to go to the game with them in Jacksonville afterwards.

Marcus went to Ohio after school went on break and then spent Christmas with the team as they practiced before travelling south. He was in constant communication with me and as usual, we made decisions together after lively discussions about almost everything.

My football playing boyfriend was a little nervous to meet my family, but I told him to stop worrying about it or I was not going to let them come to the game. He thanked me for always saying the right thing and knowing what he needed.

The Christmas break seemed boring without him, but it flew by. My brothers, Paul and Stan, my dad, and I were soon pulling into the *Holiday Inn Express* in Jacksonville. The city was abuzz with fever of the bowl game and downtown had lots of activities going on for the tourists.

I knew that I would not be seeing or hearing from Marcus until after the game, but I sent him a text anyway. I told him that we had made the trip safely and wished him good luck in the game. Needless to say, I was surprised the second night when we had just finished dinner and were walking through the bowl hospitality area when I got a text from Marcus.

You are close to me. Hilton Hotel. Meet me in the lobby restroom in five minutes.

Was his spidey sense tingling? Mine was not. *Okay*

Be safe

Yes, sir

I'm not playing, Loch

No, sir . . . I'll be safe

Hurry

I looked around and saw the Hilton on the corner ahead of us. We walked closer to it and then I said, "I'm not feeling so well. I'm going to go to the bathroom in the Hilton over there. I'll catch up with you guys in a little while."

I fended off my family's requests to help or go with me, but agreed to let them wait for me right outside. I was glad that they did not realize that the Hilton was where the football team from Carolina was staying while in Jacksonville.

The lobby of the Hilton was massive, but I spotted the restroom right away. Upon entering it, I knew my man wasn't inside because my skin and balls were not tingling. I looked, just to make sure, but he wasn't.

Maybe I got here too fast?

Walking around the lobby, I saw a bunch of kids from school and even some managers for the team. I was about to ask one of them if he had seen Marcus when I spotted another restroom on the opposite side of the grand lobby.

Quickly rushing to it, I was just inside the door when hands clamped around my mouth and eyes. Spoiling his surprise, I could feel that it was Marcus, so I relaxed in his arms and let him carry me to the furthest stall. His big chest was radiating heat against my back, even through my t-shirt.

I licked Marcus' palm that was covering my mouth just as he placed me down and uncovered my eyes. He smelled amazing and tasted even better.

"Do not turn around," he growled. His voice was so

heavily laden with lust and desire that it made me hard immediately.

"Yes, sir," I responded, partially to see if he was going to allow me to talk, and secondly, because once he was in this mood, I was unable to not submit to him. Marcus didn't order me to be quiet, which was unusual and even more thrilling to me.

"Palms on the tank," he ordered as he reached around my waist and undid the button holding up my shorts. I was bent over when he jerked my shorts and underwear down.

Marcus left the stall briefly and I was suddenly scared of what was going to happen, but he quickly returned with some liquid soap that he used as lube. I only knew that because I could smell the strong artificial ginger smell from the soap while I heard him jacking his big missile. He locked the stall door and then used one hand to stroke my back.

"You in town for the game?" Marcus asked gruffly.

What? Was this a stranger fantasy he was playing out? I can roll with that.

"Yes, sir. The Carolina team looks like a bunch of big-ass men out there. They are going to run all over Vandy."

"You're right about that," Marcus said as he ran a hand up my spine.

"What are you going to do, mister?" I asked, playing my part.

Marcus' voice was so excited when he responded that I found myself grinning like a fool against the wall. "I'm going to give you something to remember the game by, son."

"Will I like it, mister?"

"You're gonna love it," Marcus growled as he placed his hot cock head against my puckered hole and pushed his hips forward slowly. He held my hips, but I still rocked forward against the tiled wall.

"Oh, mister, it's so big," I moaned loudly.

"Don't make me gag you, son. It's just the right size for

you." Marcus pushed more of his big rod inside me.

"Hurts so good, mister," I whined.

"I'm going to shove this fat cock up so far inside you that you're gonna taste it in the back of your throat," he grunted as he pushed more and more of his mighty scepter inside me.

"Make me taste it, mister," I groaned, placing my head against the cool porcelain tiles.

"You're gonna taste my salty seed in your mouth even as late as tomorrow while you are sitting in the stands watching me plow through the Commodore defense. That is a promise, son." And with that promise, Marcus shoved his final two inches inside me and my ass was flush against his crotch.

"You're a football player, mister? That explains why your cock is so goddamn big, I guess."

"Too big for you, boy?"

"No, mister. Feels real good, punching up into me. Feels like you are fucking me with your arm."

"Your sweet hole is trying to squeeze the cum right out of my fuck stick."

"It wants you to fuck it deep and hard, mister."

"Then your tight little ass is going to get exactly what it wants," Marcus said as he pulled out of me and then sank back inside me. His thrusts began to get faster and harder, rocking me back and forth on the porcelain throne, making a terrible racket.

Suddenly Marcus slapped his big palm flat over my moaning lips and held us in place. I was gagged, impaled on Marcus' big cock, and bent over a public toilet, but I felt just as safe and content as if I was lying down in my bed.

I listened as I tried to hold my breath and regulate my heartbeat. There was some sound, and then I recognized it for what it was. Someone had come into the restroom and was now standing at one of the sinks. There was no sound of water running, so the guy must have been looking at himself in the mirror.

I gasped into his palm as Marcus pulled out of me and then slammed back inside me. He began to quietly fuck me, just as deep and hard, but not as fast as before. Listening carefully, I realized that I couldn't hear the man at the sink anymore. The door slammed open a few seconds later and someone else came into the restroom.

Marcus stopped moving and held his hand tightly over my mouth as we listened. Unbelievably, the guy went right to the mirrors and then into the stall beside us.

"What up, boys?"

The voice was right above me and I awkwardly looked up to see Finn looking over the stall wall and laughing down at us.

"Finn, get the hell out of here," Marcus snarled.

Our roommate laughed hard and loudly. "All right. You boys have fun, and I will go stand guard outside the restroom door. I'll tell them it's out of order." His steps faded towards the door, followed by the clicking of the latch as it shut behind him.

Marcus released the hand over my mouth and held onto both of my shoulders. His thick thighs moved further to the outside of mine and then he fucking ripped me a new asshole.

"Mister, you are going to make me come," I groaned as I rocked back and forth on that toilet.

"Don't come until I tell you to," he commanded me.

"Yes, sir," I said, not entirely sure that I could wait.

Marcus thrust deeply into me two more times before yelling, "Now!"

It was a good thing that he gave me permission at that point, because I was unable to hold my climax for another second. I exploded in a torrent of hot cum, coating the back of the toilet as well as some of the tiled wall.

Marcus was right behind me. He buried himself as deep

inside my ass as he could and pumped his hot sticky cum right into me.

"Filling you full of daddy's sweet seed, boy," Marcus murmured.

"Yes, sir. Fill me up, mister."

"Dropping this load right into your guts so you will remember me tomorrow, boy."

"There's no problem with that, mister. I probably won't be able to sit down during the whole game." And that statement was not just me playing a part for Marcus' benefit, but was really how I felt.

Marcus grunted with satisfaction and commanded me, "Close your eyes, boy."

I followed Marcus' order and felt him pull out of me. He smacked me on the ass, wiped himself on the roll of toilet paper on the wall, and pulled his pants up. "I'm leaving. Do not open your eyes for two minutes. Do you understand me, son?"

"Yes, sir." I actually counted to one hundred and twenty before wiping myself up, pulling on my clothes, and washing my hands. I couldn't stop smiling into the mirror as I washed up.

Exiting the restroom, I didn't see any sign of Finn or Marcus. I started to worry that I had kept my family waiting too long, so I hurried outside to re-join them in the hospitality area.

My brothers saw me coming and immediately started to walk forward. They must have been tired of waiting. I tried super-hard to not have a funny walk to compensate for the burning of my asshole. The last thing I wanted was for my family to notice that I had just been fucked.

Dad waited for me, put an arm around my back and onto my shoulder, and asked, "You okay, Loch?"

"I'm feeling a little better, thanks," I said quickly, trying to not sound so guilty.

My dad looked at me strangely and then said, "Loch, I went to the bathroom to check on you a while ago."

Oh shit!

CHAPTER TWENTY-THREE

Dad had just told me that he had checked on me in the hotel restroom where Marcus and I were having a stranger fuck. My heart was pounding out of my chest and I was frozen solid in place trying to rapidly think of how to get out of this shit storm.

"What? There were two restrooms in the lobby," I replied quickly, hoping to confuse him.

He lowered his eyes and shot me a look. "Loch, I taught you better than that. Having sex with a stranger in a hotel restroom is so risky on so many levels."

I couldn't believe that my father was able to have this discussion without getting furious. I sighed as his matter-of-factness forced me to tell the truth. "It was Marcus, Dad," I admitted.

"Even worse," he snapped, finally showing some anger. "I thought your high and mighty Marcus Battle was the man that was committed to looking after you and protecting you. Yet here he is putting you in this risky position and then leaving you alone afterwards."

"But—"

"That's not what I expected of Marcus, Loch. You told me he was different." My father was not mincing any words. He was laying it out for me whether I liked it or not.

"He is different. He would never do anything to compromise my safety," I said defensively.

"He just did," Dad said flatly. "And even more disappointing to me, you let him do it."

I wanted to tell him how strict Marcus was with me and how I had not compromised my safety for a hard fuck ever, but all of the stories ended with me getting fucking railed out, so I thought he would discount them immediately.

I was deciding what to say next when I realized that we had caught up to my brothers, who were playing a huge game of Plinko to see which team was going to win the bowl game. Dad and I couldn't continue the conversation in front of them, so we both stopped talking and started cheering on Paul and Stan.

I felt terrible that my father had just witnessed me getting fucked, that he felt Marcus and I were being risky, that I had let him down, and above all that he was questioning Marcus' commitment to protecting me. I wanted nothing more than to text or call Marcus, but I knew better than to distract him from the game.

A half hour later, I got a text from Marcus.

Thanks for that. It was fucking amazing!
It was hot . . . mister!
I wanted to hug you and tell you how hot it was after, but I didn't want to spoil the aura.
No problem. I liked that you stayed in character!
I watched you . . . afterwards. All the way back out to your family. Making sure you were safe!
I appreciate it!
You got it!
Good luck tomorrow
I'm going to try my best
No more strangers in the restroom . . .
Not until after the game . . . maybe?
Depends on your play!
Hahaha!
Hhhhmmmm . . .

My family and I were headed back to the *Holiday Inn*. I debated about whether to show Marcus' text to my father, since it refuted his statement that Marcus left me unprotected after our stranger fuck, but instead just told him that Marcus had kept an eye on me the whole time. Dad said that made him feel better, but I could tell that he still wasn't happy. What father would have been when he walked into a room where a strange man was fucking his son?

Fortunately for me, my father dropped his displeasure for the rest of the night. I was tired and went to bed early. Dreaming of a mystery man banging me in a restroom, I was soon attacked by a mass horde of NOMARs who gangbanged me like zombies eating a human. My rest was not peaceful, and I was horny as hell when I awoke.

The next morning, everyone got up early, dressed in our fan gear, and headed to a diner down the street for breakfast. The crowd was in a festive pre-game mood, and the diner was full of people dressed in Carolina blue and Vanderbilt gold. When our family and all the subsequent customers walked into the diner, the crowd from their team cheered and the other crowd groaned. It was fun to participate in and got me in the mood for the game very quickly.

Not expecting a reply, I texted Marcus to say good luck like I always did on game day. After eating, we headed to the stadium, and I introduced my brothers and father to some of the guys from school who had made the trip down for the bowl game.

Our seats were amazing, thanks to Marcus' connections, and so was the game. Carolina wound up winning at the very end, and my man had a breakout performance—scoring two touchdowns and rushing for over one hundred and fifty yards. I was super proud of him and couldn't wait to celebrate with him.

Marcus had already informed me that security was not going to let anyone come to the locker room or down into that area of the stadium, so my family just hung out where we were after the game. We talked with some of the Carolina fans around us that were letting the parking lot clear out a little before they left.

I sent a quick text to Marcus to warn him about Dad.

Hey, great game stud!

I'll show you what a stud I can be . . .

I can't wait! BTW, remember that man in the bathroom before Finn yesterday? It was my dad . . .

Oh shit . . .

I know. FYI- he's more pissed that we were at risk than he was about the fucking.

I would never put you at risk

I know. This is just like your dad thinking that I'm not good for you.

I'll deal with him

Who? Your dad or mine?

Ha-ha!

Thx

U are the reason I played so well . . .

U and that hot restroom scene!

I'm glad that I inspire you so . . .

I plan on doing it again real soon . . .

I'll be in front of the press for a while

and then I'm going to take you up on that

Marcus sent me a text telling me to come to the field a half hour later. I told my dad and the boys and we were soon down on the confetti-covered Astroturf. My tingling crotch announced Marcus' arrival before I actually saw him.

I turned around just in time to see my man coming out of the tunnel in the corner of the end zone. He looked hotter than hell in a pair of *Tommy Hilfiger* jeans, a tight-fitting V-neck light sweater in grey, and a pair of black military boots. I had never seen him in this type of outfit before, so I could only assume that he had dressed up to meet my family, and for that, I loved him so much. Of course, it didn't hurt that he looked like the man out of every one of my erotic fantasies — the giant football player, the hot bearded military commando, and the muscled construction worker dressed for a night on the town.

Having already schooled myself not to fawn over him or have a public display of affection, I checked myself, nudged my dad, nodded towards Marcus with my head, and started walking towards my boyfriend.

Marcus was the very image of a strong confident man as he spotted us and changed direction. He was tall and massively thick. He walked with an intoxicating combination of a lumber and a smooth glide. My cock was instantly on-bone, and I had to shift it in my pants just so that I could be able to continue to walk.

As we got closer, I took a moment to study the man that I had chosen to be mine more than two years ago. His handsome good looks, his freshly showered hair, his trimmed coppery beard, his square jaw, and his piercing golden eyes made him the perfect man for me. He smiled at us with perfect white teeth. The smallest thing about my big man was his mouth, so his smile always looked like he was biting his lower lip. I wanted to bite that lower lip and I wanted those lips to be on mine, crushing me.

"Loch," Marcus' deep voice boomed from a few yards away, snapping me out of my head. His voice had an uncanny knack of reverberating right through every nerve and cell in my body. I almost had to shake my head to clear it.

"Marcus Battle, I would like you to meet my father, John, and my brothers, Paul and Stan," I said, introducing them as I indicated each one of my family members in kind. I scolded myself for being so formal, but this whole situation was su-per-awkward, and now just to make it even worse, I knew that my father had seen us fucking earlier.

"I am so glad to finally meet you guys," Marcus said as he shook each one of their hands. He pumped their hands as only a big jock can and flashed them his pearly whites. He was turning on the charm and it was a thing of wonder.

"Marcus, you played a helluva game," Stan said, staring up into Marcus' face. Marcus was the tallest of all of us, but he was only an inch or so taller than me. I really didn't think of him as tall until I saw him next to shorter people like my dad and brothers. But the thing that made Marcus Battle so impos-ing was that he was so thick everywhere that it made every part of him look bigger — like a tank bearing down on you.

"Thanks, little man, but it was a team effort." Marcus turned towards Paul, smacked him in the chest, and said, "Nice jersey, guy." It was Marcus' own jersey, and we all laughed.

"You did play like a beast, Battle," my dad said, ending his quiet speculation of my favorite person on the planet.

My amazing boyfriend turned his charm onto my father and said, "Loch has told me all about you guys. It's amazing that you were able to come to the game and support us."

"It was our pleasure," Dad told him. He turned towards me, lowered his voice and mumbled, "And obviously yours as well."

Marcus took the snide remark and turned it around by say-ing, "It is my pleasure to have you guys come and root for me and the team. Maybe it is what inspired me today," he said smoothly while noticeably turning his attention to me. "And I know that Loch appreciates you being here."

I blushed so hard and fast that I thought my skin might have caught fire.

There was an awkward silence, and then my dad covered

it smoothly. "We were just going to grab something to eat. Would you like to go to dinner with us, Marcus, or do you have to stay with the team?" my dad asked.

Suddenly, it occurred to me that my father had been a football coach when he first started working, and he probably had always wanted a son like Marcus. I mean, who wouldn't? Instead, he got me. I was more academically inclined, but was still a pretty decent athlete. But, no matter what my strengths were, I was still the one taking it up the ass from someone he probably would have rather sired.

"I would be honored, John."

"We'll be the ones with the star of the game at our table," Paul said. I recognized the look of awe in my brother's eyes, because it was the same one that I usually had in mine when looking at Marcus Battle.

"The star," I repeated with a raised eyebrow at the big football player standing beside me. My Marcus was just as humble as he was talented and he flushed bright pink at the praise. "I'm just picking on you, you big lug. Of course you were the star, and we will all be honored with your presence at our table."

Marcus hooked my head in the crook of his arm with a lightning fast move. The electrical charge that flowed between us when our skin touched was on full display as my body reacted to him. He smelled amazing and I wanted nothing else in the world but to lick him from head to toe. I watched in amazement as Dad chuckled and turned to leave.

"Drag him this way, Marcus," my father said loudly as he pushed my two brothers ahead of him.

Chapter Twenty-Four

My family, Marcus and I had walked to a steak restaurant near the stadium that was surprisingly not crowded, considering that we were the last to leave the game. The manager recognized Marcus right away, and we were soon seated and getting the royal treatment.

Everyone was discussing the game and was interested in Marcus' stories and comments. A man soon came over and asked for Marcus' autograph, which he graciously gave while not even interrupting the story he was telling. The rest of us were digging into the free appetizers that had been delivered to our table.

My dad had convinced Marcus and me to join him in drinking beers, so both of us ordered one. I hoped that it would mellow my father out a little, and it certainly wouldn't be bad for my nerves.

The food soon arrived, and the conversation ebbed while everyone tucked into their steaks and potatoes. I was so engrossed in cutting into my filet that I didn't even notice that there was a man standing at our table until he reached across me and handed Marcus a program. I was sitting beside Marcus but the man was standing beside me. I could smell the alcohol on him as well as his perspiration.

"Could you?" he mumbled to Marcus. Our whole table's attention was now on the intruder.

Marcus looked at him in annoyance and asked, "Do you have a pen?"

The drunk man dug in his pocket and found a flair pen

which he dropped in my plate. I handed it to Marcus who signed the program quickly and handed it back to him. I assumed it was over, but instead the drunk guy nudged me with his hand that was gripping the pen and program.

"What?" I asked as I looked up at him. He was really starting to annoy me now.

He indicated his hand and it hit me that he wanted me to sign the program. "I'm not a player," I said loudly with a smile to the rest of the table.

The drunk guy stumbled towards Marcus and then righted himself and shifted to the other side of the table, diagonally from me behind Seth. He took a look my way, squinted, and then his eyes cleared slightly.

"You're a goddamn cocksucker!" he said loudly as he took in my mark. He turned to my father and said, "Hey mister, you must be proud because your son is a football star and he's got his own cum bucket to boot."

I winced at the words as much as the looks of all of the other patrons who had stopped talking and now were busy staring.

"I'm actually the cum bucket's father," my dad said with a smile towards me.

Marcus was not so nice. He was on his feet in a blur of grey. Before I could even register what was happening, Marcus had his hand around the drunk guy's throat and he was in his face. "You will apologize."

The drunk guy gurgled out a laugh and asked, "For what?"

"For being a drunken asshole who is not half the man that the marked guy is," Marcus turned to the side slightly so that the drunk could see me again.

The drunk started to say, "Half the man—"

"I will break your fucking neck," Marcus growled in a voice that I had only heard when his big cock was buried to the hilt inside me. He tightened his grip.

"I'm sorry," the drunk immediately said to me.

"And now to his father," Marcus commanded.

"Sorry, Dad."

"And to his brothers," Marcus growled.

"No fucking way!" the drunk yelled.

"Do it," Marcus ordered while squeezing harder. He did not even raise his voice, but his tone was scary regardless.

"I'm sorry," he finally said.

Marcus got even closer to the intruder's face and said, "Now, get the fuck out of here before I beat you down in front of all these nice people." With that, Marcus dragged the drunk around the table and threw him towards the front door.

The manager was waiting there to escort the drunk out. The patrons clapped for Marcus, but he ignored them as he checked on me and regained his seat.

"You okay, Loch?" he asked, his penetrating golden gaze locked onto my green ones.

"I am. Thanks, Marcus."

"Yes, thanks Marcus," my dad said. I looked over at my father and I saw a new look on his face as he looked at my protector — admiration.

"It was only what you would have done, sir, or Loch for that matter. I was just keeping either one of you from having to dirty your hands."

"It was awesome, Marcus," my brothers said in unison. They were both taken by my over-sized boyfriend.

My father finally stopped looking at Marcus and turned to me. "Is he always so quick to defend you, Loch?"

"He's usually quicker. I guess he is off his game a little." I chuckled as I speared a piece of my steak with my fork.

"I was just waiting to see how your father was going to handle it," Marcus said, grinning as he chewed a piece of steak himself.

"It was impressive nonetheless," my dad interjected. "I think you may have chosen wisely, Loch."

"I know I did," I said as everything in my world righted itself again.

Months later, I looked back on that night as something of a turning point in my relationship with Marcus. It was not for us so much as for how my family perceived us. Marcus was now considered to be part of the family, like a rock star to my brothers and like a long lost son to my dad. They constantly asked how he was and sent texts for me to invite him home every time I was heading that way.

I eventually took them up on the offer, and Marcus joined me in Charleston for spring break. I thought it might have been awkward when we arrived that night, but they seemed to have it all worked out.

"Should I put our stuff in my old room?" I asked my dad as I indicated our bags. I had always shared a room with Paul which he had now taken over. That room had two twin beds in it and it would have killed me if I'd had to sleep that close to Marcus Battle without being able to touch him.

Dad said, "No, Stan has moved into Paul's bedroom for the week and I'm going to stay in Stan's room for the week."

I almost laughed out loud because I thought they were pranking me. "What?" I finally asked when I saw that my dad was serious.

"My bed is bigger and you guys can have the privacy of it and the separate bath," my father explained.

I looked at Marcus and raised an eyebrow.

Did my father actually expect me to sleep with Marcus under his roof and even more shocking – did he expect us to fuck? I mean, we were going to anyway, but I didn't want it to be a publicly accepted fact.

That question was answered the next day after I had given Marcus the quietest blowjob in history. My brothers were out and my father had made breakfast for Marcus and me when we finally rolled out of bed.

Dad sat at the table with us as we ate, making the whole experience a little weird. He asked what our plans were for the day and Marcus told him that he was going to work out and then I was going to show him around Charleston. I agreed that I would help Dad with a home repair project he was working on while Marcus was lifting weights.

Marcus had just changed clothes and headed to the gym. It was down the street from the house and I had already pointed it out to him, so there was no reason for me to go with him.

As soon as Marcus left for the gym, Dad pulled me to the side. "You and Marcus fuck last night?"

"Dad!" I said in disbelief.

"What?" he asked with his hands spread to his sides.

I stared at him in disbelief. "First, it's none of your business and second, when did this become okay with you?"

"I like Marcus," he said plainly.

"And?"

"And, I think you two are good together."

"And?" I prompted again.

"I don't want you to lose him."

I balked at that. "Why would I lose him?"

He reached over the table and grasped my shoulder. "Son, I know I taught you how to handle yourself and how to avoid danger, but we never had the talk about everything else."

"Everything else?"

Dad continued, "It never really occurred to me that you would find someone who you would respect and love."

I blushed at his words.

He added, "So, I never talked with you about how not to lose someone like that."

"What are you talking about?" I asked in exasperation.

"A man like that needs to fuck, Loch."

I was shocked to hear that come out of my father's mouth, but I stared at him because it just had.

"And he needs to fuck a lot. If you don't let him, he will look elsewhere."

"Where else would he look?" I challenged him.

"Loch, your boyfriend is a star. He is going to the NFL and will soon be very wealthy and very famous. He can just call for a Servant or take home a dozen of the marked men who will flock to every one of his games after he leaves Carolina."

This information struck me like a blow and I realized that I was holding my breath. I didn't want to believe what he was saying, but I knew in my heart that it was true. All year, I had noticed that Marcus was on that path, and I dreaded where it was heading.

My father's face softened when he saw my reaction to his words. "If you want to keep him, Loch, you must make him happy."

"I do make him happy," I whined.

"You are both growing boys who need to drain your nuts in order to maintain good health. Marcus is a bull. I can see that. He probably has so much cum in his nuts that he can't possibly get rid of it all."

I chuckled. "He certainly tries to drain them at every chance."

"That's good. Let him, Loch." He stopped suddenly and looked hard at me. "You do enjoy it, don't you, Loch?"

"Very much."

"Good. I can tell that you love him and I hoped that meant that you love the sex also. And if I know you, you are probably the aggressor nine times out of ten."

I laughed and said, "Surprisingly, we are about equal in that department."

"I can't believe that I'm saying this to my son, but let Marcus fuck you as much as he wants, Loch. Be something new for him, be exciting, be fun to be around, don't hover or whine when he wants to go out, be a refuge for him at the end of his day . . ."

I looked at my father like he had two heads, because I knew that I was doing all the right things already. The only part that worried me was the future after school. Marcus and I had never discussed it, because he never verbalized any hopes or dreams about playing in the NFL. I figured it was a superstitious thing for him.

"I'm doing my best, Dad."

"I'm sure you are, Loch. You've always made me proud of you."

"Thanks, Dad. I can't believe that we are even having this conversation . . ."

"It's not the future I wanted for you, Loch. But I've always tried to do my best with what you brought to the table and always do right by you. I feel like Marcus Battle might be your best option."

I squinted my eyes and turned my head slightly towards him. "My best option at what?"

"Happiness, of course."

I was taken aback by that and struck silent.

Dad exhaled and explained, "Loch, all I've ever dreamed for you was for safety, but now I see that you have a chance at something better, something bigger, something in addition to safety."

"Okay . . ."

"But you have to cultivate it, Loch. You picked a good one when you picked Marcus Battle, but you have to groom him."

If only you knew how much I have groomed him . . .

"How do you know I picked him?"

"Well, didn't you? You're the boy I raised, so I just assumed that you picked the biggest, best stud in the corral."

"I was actually one of the smallest, meekest studs in the corral," Marcus' deep voice boomed from the living room. He appeared a few seconds later, and my father blushed a deep red when he realized Marcus might have overheard what he had been saying.

"I-I find that hard to believe," my dad stammered as he looked up and down at the mountain of man that Marcus was in his work-out gear. He was hot and sweaty and his muscles were pulsing with blood and adrenaline, making them hard as rocks and shiny under the sheen of sweat.

Marcus turned one of the chairs at the table around and sat down with us. "Believe it or not, John, I was a scrawny freshman who was afraid to say boo in the locker room that freshman season. Your son saw something in me that I hadn't even seen yet. He cultivated it, nursed it, coaxed it, and even sometimes enticed it out of me. Loch is absolutely as much responsible for the man that I am today as I am. So, you see, he doesn't have to cultivate me or my happiness because he has already spent three years grooming me into who I am today." Marcus turned towards me with his penetrating golden eyes and added, "And I have to think that he has done the same thing for *us* — making us better together."

Marcus turned back towards my father and said, "You raised an amazing man, John, and he's going to get everything he deserves."

It was a fantastic speech that left me with a swollen heart and a huge hard-on. Marcus was absolutely not afraid to express how he felt about me, no matter whom he was talking to, and that was a real turn-on for me.

Dad nodded his head positively and said, "Good."

"Well, I'm ready to get some of what I deserve," I said like a smart ass, looking from my father to my boyfriend. I stood up and held out my hand to Marcus.

Marcus looked confused and a little baffled why I would be so blatant in front of my father, but he took my hand and stood up. He let me guide him towards the bedroom.

"Have fun," my dad called after us.

I pulled my boyfriend into the bedroom and shut the door.

"What the hell?" Marcus asked.

"He wants you to fuck me." I chuckled.

Marcus looked like he had been shot. "He said that?"

"That and a lot more," I said as I stripped. "He's not going to be happy until we put on a show."

"We can do that," Marcus said, grinning from ear to ear.

"Yes, we can!"

CHAPTER TWENTY-FIVE

"You want me to shower first?" Marcus asked gruffly.

"Can you resist this for ten more minutes," I asked as I turned my ass towards him and bent forward slightly. I knew he had been without it for more than twenty-four hours and he was probably dying.

"No," he answered bluntly.

"Let's go then, stud," I said, chuckling.

Marcus was on me in a heartbeat. He pressed his big sweaty body up against me and his lips found mine. He kissed me like he hadn't seen me in months and I returned his fervor.

When I was finally able to disconnect from his hungry mouth, I jumped into his arms and wrapped my long legs around his waist. Marcus supported my back while I locked my arms around his thick neck and he carried us towards the bed. His big erection was nestled between my buns until he threw me down onto the bed.

I unlocked my arms and legs and fell onto my back.

"You brought lube?" Marcus whispered.

"Let's skip it," I said with a raised eyebrow.

Marcus jerked his head up to me. "Really?"

"You're sweaty, aren't you?"

"Fucking straight."

"Then spear me with that claw, you big bear," I said, grinning foolishly at him. My body was ringing like a bell, between the electric connection between the two of us and my anticipation of what was about to happen.

"You are a constant surprise, but I don't want to hurt you," Marcus said softly.

"Stop being such a goddamn gentleman and give me the hard fuck my daddy wants you to," I encouraged him snarkily.

"Maybe this will shut you up," Marcus mumbled as he speared my asshole with his big cock head and shoved his hips forward. His cock penetrated me like it had done thousands of times before, but this time it did not slide in so easily.

It did shut me up as I gasped in pain and squeezed my eyes shut.

"You okay, Loch?"

"Give me a second . . ."

Marcus pushed us back into the middle of the bed, leaned all the way over me, and was staring down at me when I opened my eyes. "We don't have to do this, Loch. Won't it be more enjoyable for you if I lube myself?"

"You know me better than that, don't you, Battle?" I countered. I reached up, took hold of his massive biceps, lifted myself up, and then impaled myself all the way down on his massive pike. I let out a huge groan as my ass cheeks settled into Marcus' lap.

"Or you could do that," he said, grinning like a fool down at me. "You like the way it feels?"

"I do. More than you will ever know." I paused for a second, considering him. Suddenly, I blurted out, "Do I make you happy, Marcus?"

He looked down at me in confusion and said, "More than you will ever know, Loch, more than you will ever know." He bent to my face and kissed me hard as he began to pump his big cock back and forth inside of me.

Marcus lifted above me and really began to fuck me hard. I lifted my mouth to his ear and said, "Let's make sure Daddy hears it, huh Master?"

Marcus raised both eyebrows and I nodded my consent as I lay my back down on the mattress and arched it so that my boyfriend could have total access to my already-burning hole.

Marcus Battle pounded me so hard and fast that the head-board of the bed began to bang the bedroom wall. We made quite a ruckus, and by the time we each reached our climax, Marcus was pile-driving me into the mattress with such force that we broke the slats out of Dad's bed and collapsed into a hole in the middle.

Marcus landed on top of me just as he released his seed deep inside my anal chamber. My eruption happened just as his sweaty chest smashed me. My cock pumped sticky hot cum between our sweaty bodies as I tried to catch my breath.

"Thanks for that," Marcus whispered to me.

"No need to whisper now," I said, chuckling.

Later, I went to soak in a tub of hot water. I could overhear Marcus and my father talking through the open door.

My father asked, "Where's Loch?"

"He's soaking in the tub," Marcus answered. I could hear the apprehension in his voice and held my breath as I waited to hear what my father wanted.

"Oh."

"John, you are going to need to shore that bed up, if you want us to come back," Marcus said to my father, laughing so hard that he almost couldn't get it out.

"Loch take care of you?"

"Take care of me? He fucking drained me three times. Your son is really an amazing man, John."

"Yes, he is. And that's why I'm so protective of him."

"So am I, John, so am I."

The rest of our spring break was fun and relaxing. My boy-friend and my father worked on repairing the bed together, talking and laughing the whole time. I was grateful that they were getting along, so I tried to stay out of their way and let them bond.

Marcus and I returned to Chapel Hill and almost immediately fell into the last rush of classes and final exams. We took the Saturday before our first exam to spend the day entirely with each other. I knew that we needed to have a talk about the summer and about senior year, but I was already dreading being away from him, and this talk would signify the start of that separation, so I couldn't bring myself to have it.

Marcus woke me early on Saturday and sent me to the store to buy food for four meals—two breakfasts, one lunch, and one dinner, plus snacks. I wanted to ask why, but Marcus put his pointer finger up to his lips and shook his head ever so slightly. His actions and the mystery behind them piqued my curiosity and made me very excited.

I threw on some clothes and practically ran to the grocery store. It had just opened, which Marcus probably knew, and I quickly bought everything I thought we might want to eat for the day. When I returned to the house, Marcus already had his military-style knapsack packed and was carrying it to his truck.

"Put the groceries in here," he commanded, indicating the back of his truck.

I followed his order and saw a case of water already there. "Where are we going, stud?"

Marcus didn't answer, but held up a set of keys instead. He shook them slightly and I realized that they were the keys that belonged to one of the football booster's houses near campus. It was the site of our first date, and later, our first fuck. My heart started to beat faster and I couldn't help but grin from ear-to-ear.

"You approve, Loch?"

"Fuck, yes!"

"Get in the truck," he ordered.

I could tell by the heaviness of his voice that Marcus was already turned on. This would probably be the last chance we would have to be relaxed before finals week started, and then afterwards we would be separated again, so today was very special for both of us.

Marcus drove us in silence to the booster's house, although he kept his big paw on the inside of my thigh the whole trip. I used the time to tickle and examine his meaty arm and hand with my fingers as he drove. He growled at me a couple of times, but did not tell me to stop. I was absolutely hard as a rock when we arrived and parked on the street in front of the beautiful Dutch colonial house.

Grabbing all the bags of groceries at once, I watched as Marcus put the strap of the knapsack around his broad shoulders and then lifted the case of water onto one shoulder like it weighed nothing. He looked completely edible in a black tank top and green cargo shorts.

We carried our loads to the front door, where Marcus indicated for me to put them down.

"Loch," he said lustily. It was amazing what his voice could do to me with one single word. Of course, it helped that the word was my name. That word alone carried so much weight and promise that I could hardly stand the importance of it.

"Yes, Master?" I could tell that this experience was going to be one for the record books, which meant that Marcus was going to dominate me like I wanted to be. He enjoyed it just as much as I did, and the fact that we didn't get to engage in these roles very often just made the times when we did even more special.

He immediately sucked in his breath. "You make me so fucking hot for you," he said as he placed an oversized hand on my mark and ran his big rough thumb across my cheek to my lips.

"I can't even put into words what you do for me, Master."

"I can see," he smirked as his hand dropped down to my crotch and he tweaked my hard cock that was poking out of my silky basketball shorts.

I blushed furiously even though over the past three years, there was nothing that he hadn't done to me or known about me.

Marcus held up the keys and said, "Loch, when we enter this house, you will not speak again until you are directed to do so. Do you understand?"

"Yes, sir." There was nothing in the universe hotter than Marcus Battle going into what I called Master-mode. His command and dominance of me was the ultimate turn-on.

"You will only use my title. That is the one word that you are permitted to say without being directed to. If you disobey, you will be gagged. Do you understand?"

"Yes, Master."

"When we enter this house, you will follow my directives without fail. Do you understand?"

"Yes, sir."

"You will do nothing without my permission or order. Do you understand?"

"Yes, Master."

"If you fail to comply with these rules, you will be severely punished, Loch. Do you understand?"

I gulped hard, knowing that this was going to be difficult for me. I was headstrong and independent. Not a good combination for a Servant. Suddenly, I was terrified when the thought that the punishment might be that he wouldn't fuck me crossed my mind. "Yes, Master."

"You will not disappoint me, Loch," he said firmly.

"No, Master."

"You are my Servant, at least for the next twenty-four

hours, Loch." Marcus' voice was so deep and lusty that I thought he might be reaching his climax right there on the front porch in front of the still-locked door.

"I am your Servant."

"And who am I?"

"You are my Master."

"And who do you belong to?"

"You, Master."

"And who knows what you need, what you desire, and what you want?"

"You do, Master."

"And who is going to give you what you need?"

"You will, Master."

"And what is it that you want more than anything else?"

"You, Master." I wasn't just playing a role. For me, it was real and true. There was nothing that I wanted more than Marcus Battle.

"And what are you willing to do to have me?"

"Anything, Master."

"Anything I desire, Servant?"

"Yes, Master. Your desires are all that matter to me. I only desire to make your desires reality."

"Show me."

I wasn't sure what he meant for me to do. I knew that I was supposed to wait for his directives, but he said that was when we had entered the house. Finally after looking deep into his eyes and weighing my options, I slowly lowered myself to the welcome mat in front of the door and unzipped the fly of his cargo shorts. Reaching in, I pulled his massive hard-on out through the fly. Marcus' cock was hot as fire and already had a drop of golden man-goo nestled in the piss slit.

"Loch," he said with awe in his voice.

"Master," I said, echoing his tone.

My eyes shifted to the street. We were completely exposed

to the neighborhood, but I realized that it didn't matter. If someone told me that I had to debase myself in front of a public audience in order to show Marcus how much he meant to me, then I would have completely done it. There would have been no question.

Softly, I ran the tips of my fingers up the long hard shaft, exploring the thick veins that bulged out from his skin. The electric charge that normally ran through me in Marcus' presence intensified when our skins touched, and this moment was no exception to that rule. Suddenly, the world collapsed into two people and a door mat—everything else fell away, and I wasn't even aware of being in public or having any other feeling than complete adoration for my man.

I flicked my tongue out and captured that drop of his delicious pre-cum from the pinnacle of his magnificent cock. I swallowed it and then held his cock up to his body so that I could run my tongue from his low-hanging balls all the way up his shaft.

Marcus groaned from somewhere deep inside his chest and put his big hand on the top of my head. His fingers were splayed out, and he was soon controlling me like I was a remote-controlled blowing machine. He clearly wanted his cock inside my mouth, and I was not going to fight it.

I swallowed him in one giant gulp. His large cockhead blasted the back of my mouth and my spittle ran out over the base of that long prong as I choked on it. Marcus held me there as he enjoyed the wet heat engulfing his hot prick.

When he released the pressure on my head, I began to pump my mouth up and down on his big cock, using my tongue and lips to bring him to the edge of his climax. Pulling on his balls, I took turns licking on the outside of his shaft and pistoning my mouth up and down on him.

Marcus grunted loudly and then let out a low moan as he fell over the edge of his climax. He pulled his cock out of my mouth with one hand while he pushed my head away from him with the other. Wrapping his big hand around his shaft right below the foreskin of his cockhead, he pointed the cum vent right at my face as he erupted.

Hot sticky cum hit me in the eye and nose with more than a little force. I closed my eyes automatically, but kept my mouth open as one ropy strand after another coated my face and dripped into my mouth.

"Fuck!" Marcus roared as he pumped more and more of his man seed onto my face.

I used my tongue to wipe as much of it off of my face as I could reach, but to no avail, because Marcus was intent on giving me a cum mask to wear. He applied layer after layer of his thick cream to my mask.

"Oh, my fucking God," Marcus mumbled as he came back to himself. He reached down and used both big thumbs to wipe my eyes off. Inserting both of his thumbs into my mouth, I sucked them clean.

That was when we both noticed that we were being watched. A noise went up from the street and I blinked to see that a group of college kids had taken a seat on the stone wall across the street and were now clapping and whooping their excitement to us.

One of them stood up and yelled while grabbing his crotch, "Hey man, you gonna share that mouth with us?"

Marcus pulled me to my feet. "No way in hell!" he yelled to the boys. "Get one of these for yourself."

"That's not fair," another guy yelled.

Marcus looked at me and shrugged his shoulders. I could see this turning ugly, so I needed to put a stop to it.

"Any of you got a dick this big?" I asked with a smirk as I held Marcus' still-hard cock in the palm of my hand. It looked like a flesh-colored fire hose. I raised it into the air just in case they couldn't see the baby arm from where they were sitting.

When nothing but silence was the response, I said, "Sorry, boys."

Marcus laughed out loud and unlocked the front door. I stepped inside to the place I desired to be more than anywhere else on earth.

CHAPTER TWENTY-SIX

Once we were inside the door of the booster's house, Marcus closed it behind him. He looked at me with such longing that it made my heart break.

"Do you hate me for that, Loch?"

I shook my head, remembering his orders.

"Do you feel debased or humiliated? I want you to tell me the truth."

I repeated my gesture and he let out a huge sigh of relief.

"You know that I would hate myself for it, if I ever made you feel that way. Speak, Loch."

"I would do anything for you, Master. I would follow your commands no matter what they were." As soon as I said it, I wondered if the words were true.

Would I do that?

"If I am debased, then it is for a purpose and it is not my purview to necessarily know what that purpose is. I don't really care what the purpose, is because my only goal is to satisfy your commands."

He reached out and touched me again on the face. "You trust me that much, Loch?"

I nodded my head.

"I am honored to be with you," Marcus said with feeling. He pulled himself up straight and dropped his hand. "Now, go clean yourself up while I put the groceries away."

I turned on my heel immediately and headed to the downstairs bathroom. I had been in this house multiple times and knew it like the back of my hand.

When I emerged from the bathroom with a clean face, Marcus was just throwing away the grocery bags. He looked at me and said, "Good. Which would you like to do first, Servant, make us breakfast or get pounded by my breakfast sausage?"

I didn't know how to answer without speaking and was just about ready to perform some charades when he added, "Loch, you are making me very happy with your silence. You may answer now."

"I would like you to fuck me hard, Master."

"Excellent," he said, smiling. "Then we shall eat. Please make us something good, Loch, while I put our bag in the bedroom."

I looked at him with a questioning look and he immediately returned my look with a hard stare and a raised eyebrow of his own.

Note to self — choose the opposite next time.

I had already planned out breakfast while I was shopping, so it didn't take me long to whip up toast with eggs in the middle, fresh cantaloupe, and sausage patties. Marcus was eating a lot lately, as he had increased his workouts for football. His workouts with me remained steady and vigorous as always.

He was soon back in the kitchen, where he sat down at the table and watched me work. Marcus began to whistle, but never took his eyes off of me. I wondered what he was thinking behind that big goofy grin of his, but knew better than to ask.

I served him his plate of food, which was twice as much as mine, and took the chair across from him.

"Thank you, my Servant," he said as he dug into the plate of food.

I passed him the salt and pepper and watched as he used the salt lightly and the pepper heavily. He took big bites of everything, swallowed it, and complimented me on it all.

Continuing to watch Marcus the entire time he ate, I saw that he had a good appetite and seemed to really enjoy my cooking, so I was very pleased with myself. When he finished, he sat back in his chair and patted his stomach.

"That was excellent, Loch. Now, would you like me to give you that hard fuck you wanted or would you like to clean these dishes and pans?"

Remembering to pick the opposite of what I wanted, I picked up my dirty plate and indicated it.

"You want to clean up?" he asked with a smirk and a raised eyebrow.

I couldn't help but smile as I nodded in the affirmative.

"You may."

I stared at him in dismay.

"You have something to say, Servant?" Marcus challenged me.

I slowly shook my head from side to side this time.

"Good. I will wait for you in the bedroom. And Servant, do not keep me waiting any longer than I desire."

"Master," I said as I bowed my head.

"Good boy," Marcus told me as he tousled my hair and headed out of the kitchen.

I felt pressure to go to him quickly, so I scurried about the kitchen, loading the dishwasher and putting away the leftover food. I couldn't help but wonder if this is what life after school would be if Marcus became my true Master. I told myself that Marcus would not make me do all the cooking and cleaning in the real world, that he was just doing it today for this scenario, but I didn't know for sure.

Would this become my life? And would I want it to be my life?

Whatever my mind was deciding, my body had already made up its mind, because my cock was hard as a fucking two-by-four. I dried my hands and practically ran up the stairs to the master bedroom. Sensing his electrical charge before I rounded the corner, I entered the bedroom to see

Marcus Battle spread out diagonally across the bed. He was propped up on one arm and was reading a *Sports Illustrated*. It was a beautiful sight, and I stopped dead in my tracks as I took in the sight of him.

"Ah, my Servant. I was just getting ready to call for you."

I licked my lips in anticipation.

"Undress. You will not wear clothes again as long as we are here. Do you understand, Servant?"

I nodded that I understood even as I pulled off my t-shirt and stepped out of my basketball shorts. My underwear was not far behind.

"Undress me," Marcus commanded.

Going around to the opposite side of the bed, I pulled the hem of his tank top up and over his gorgeous chest and head. Marcus had not showered that morning and the smell of his masculine body almost made me lightheaded. My cock was already so painfully hard, and now I was just torturing myself with the sight of Marcus' body in my eyes, the touch of his skin under my fingers, and his smell in my nostrils.

With shaking fingers I moved down to the button of the cargo shorts at his waist. Soon I had his shorts off and was carefully pulling down his boxer briefs to reveal the dick of my dreams.

"Do you like my body, Servant?" he asked me with a voice so husky that it threatened to set me on fire.

I nodded that I did.

"Do you like my cock, Servant?"

I repeated my gesture.

"Tell me how much, Servant."

"It is mine, Master. It is as much a part of me as my own cock, Master."

He chuckled. "It certainly has been inside you more than anything else in the world."

I nodded my agreement.

"Would you like it inside you now, Servant?"

I dropped my game plan to try to manipulate him and answered honestly by nodding my head in the affirmative.

"Very good, Servant. I am committed to give you what you need, Loch. The first two times that I asked your opinion, you were still trying to manipulate me or give me what you thought I wanted. It is refreshing to get an honest answer out of you."

I couldn't help but look hurt.

"I didn't mean to imply that you aren't honest, Servant, because I think you are, but I do like when I know what you truly feel instead of you trying to please me. It is important for both of us to get what we need and want. I never want to take advantage of you, and I would never forgive myself if I was getting more pleasure from our relationship than you were getting for yourself."

That made me feel better, and I moved towards his big cock to blow him for saying it. Marcus immediately held up his index finger and wagged it back and forth, stopping me in my tracks.

"Tell me how I want you, Servant."

I knew the answer just like he had asked me for my name. "You want me to lie down on top of you, Master."

"Yes, I do. Lube me, and then I can be inside you where you need me to be, Servant."

"Master," I responded as I spotted the tube of lube on the nightstand. I squirted it into my palm and then stroked his glorious member with such focus that it was like I was polishing a sacred relic. I never really had to rub him up hard, because hard was Marcus' natural state.

As soon as I had him lubed, he pulled himself up into a sitting position and commanded, "Lay down on the bed beside me so your feet are up here." He indicated the mattress beside his chest.

This is unusual. We've never done this before.

I followed his command and he pulled my legs up further. "Lay back, my Servant."

I did and watched as Marcus lowered his feet down onto my face. He was gentle, and I was careful to keep my tongue in my mouth, even though my first instinct was to grab his dogs and give them a complete foot bath.

Marcus exhaled and said, "Servant, you are making me so proud of you. You dedication to following my rules will not go unrewarded." He rubbed my face with the bottoms of his feet and explored my lips with his big toes.

"You may show your love for my feet now, Servant," he said, allowing me to lick and kiss his size-fourteen feet. I didn't know whether I was allowed to touch them with my hands, but I couldn't help it, so I grabbed both of his feet and held them in place as I completely coated them in my saliva.

I had just sucked all his toes and currently had both of his big toes in my mouth at the same time when Marcus said, "You really love my feet, don't you big guy?"

I nodded with my mouth full of his toes.

"I'm sorry I haven't been able to feed them to you recently, but I had a case of athlete's foot from the locker room that I had to get rid of first. The team doc just cleared me yesterday."

I didn't care. I loved sucking on every part of Marcus Battle, and if I got some kind of something by doing it, then that was why they made antibiotics.

Marcus looked at me with adoration and said, "Fuck, you would do anything I asked you to do, wouldn't you?"

Removing his toes from my mouth, I smiled, bowed my head, and said, "Master."

"Get up here. I need to be inside you right now." Marcus' voice had become lusty and ragged.

I scrambled up to my feet, straddled his crotch, and lowered my ass down to it. Marcus guided his big cock head to my puckered hole and then punched it inside.

Gasping from the sudden pain, I tried to concentrate on how fantastic it felt to have my anal ring spread so completely apart. Marcus rubbed a large palm up my spine to try to relax me.

Taking a deep breath and exhaling it slowly, I ground my ass down on the rest of his giant telephone pole that normally swung between his legs. His cock head plunged deep into my guts, clearing my baffles and giving me that full feeling that I loved so much. My asshole stretched around his girthy shaft, feeling every raised vein along the way and squeezing him tightly.

"That's it, baby. Open up and let your Master in." Marcus was gliding me down with his hands on my hips, but he now moved his hands to my ass cheeks. He spread them wide open, and I could just envision him watching that big meat pole of his slide into me.

"Fuck me! I love being right there," Marcus groaned as he reached the bottom of my mine shaft. "Your ass is just as tight as the day we first fucked."

I groaned to show my agreement.

"Come down here to me, Servant," Marcus said as he pulled on my shoulders and dropped me to his chest. He held me in place by wrapping his long muscled arms around my stomach, and then his feet hooked over the top of my ankles. I was securely bound to him, just like I had been for the last three years.

"There, now that's better. Loch, I would like you to talk with me now."

Marcus' cock was throbbing deep inside my ass like a ticking time bomb. "Yes, Master," I immediately acknowledged.

"What are your plans for the summer, Loch?" he asked as he brushed my hard nipple with the palm of one of his hands.

"I will need to return to Charleston and work at IBM as usual, Master. Will you be going to Oregon this summer?"

"No, I'm going to stay here and work with the coaches. I was hoping that you could stay with me."

"I wish, but if I don't work at IBM for the summer, then I won't get my scholarship. And Dad really needs that."

"I understand. I was just being selfish."

"I can come visit you on the weekends, maybe."

"That would be cool," Marcus said as he wrapped his long fingers around my hard dick. He began to pump the skin of my cock back and forth over the hard core. "Will you live with me again next year, Loch?"

"Yes, of course, Master."

"Good. I have enjoyed living with you."

"Me, too, Master."

Is he is planning ahead? Would he consider living with me after graduation? My mind was swimming with the possibilities, but the huge throbbing cock buried deep inside me was taking my focus away from truly being able to concentrate on these questions.

My boyfriend continued his questioning of me by asking, "Will you continue your affair with Mr. Lewellyn over the summer?"

"I think I have to in order to not nullify my agreement with him concerning my scholarship."

"Yes, I think you will, too."

"Do you hate me for it?" I asked cautiously. I had always wondered how Marcus truly felt about me sleeping around during the summer, even though it was at his urging that I first started.

"Why would you ask that?"

"Because your father thinks I'm a whore for sleeping around and making you constantly worry about who is drilling me," I answered bluntly. I had been waiting to tell him this nugget, but immediately regretted how pointedly I did it.

"Of course I don't hate you, Loch, and my father is wrong about you. It keeps you safe and even. Do I like it? Of course not. I want to keep you full of my cock around the clock, but since I can't over the summer, this will have to do."

I could hear the honesty in his voice with just a twinge of something behind it. "It will be the last time, at least." I saw my chance and decided to take it. "Master?"

"Yes, Loch?"

"What will happen next year? For us, I mean."

"Let's not think about that now, Loch."

"Yes, sir," I said, trying to keep the disappointment out of my voice.

"Do you still trust me, Loch?"

"With my life, Master."

"Then you trust that I will do what is best for you?"

"I do, Master."

"Good. Then whatever happens next year at this time, it will be the thing that is best for both of us."

"Yes, sir," I answered, wondering if I could live with the decision he would make or not. I guess that I would have to . . .

"I know you are disappointed, Loch, but we have a whole year of fun ahead of us if we don't get too wrapped up in everything else. Doesn't that sound good?"

"Yes, Master. I will try my best to not worry about it." I could hear my father's voice in my head reminding me to be fun-loving and easy for Marcus.

"Will it help if I keep you bound to my bed for the entire year? Because that thought has crossed my mind."

I could feel the excitement in his cock and hear it in his voice after he had asked me. "It will!" I said with enthusiasm.

"I wish," he said, chuckling. "Now, to get down to business. Who do you belong to, Loch?"

"I belong to you, Master."

"You are mine."

"I am yours. And you are mine, Master."

"I am yours," he replied instantly.

I was reassured by this simple equation that we had with each other. And, of course, by the extremely hard fuck session that Marcus Battle bestowed on me over the next twenty-four hours. Marcus and I were bound to each other in every possible way.

But our future together was still unresolved . . .

YOU MAY ALSO ENJOY THE FOLLOWING FROM EXTASY BOOKS INC:

Phantom Master
Crawford Rhine

Excerpt

I had planned to stay in my hotel room today, but now I was itching to get out and about. I had Googled the Madsen Theater and the newspaper stories of the horrible electrical accident that happened there. The rising country star was named Truck McPherson and he was hot as shit in his pictures. I had read everything I could find on all those subjects and nothing had deterred me from liking the place as much as I already did.

I showered and got ready in a hurry. I threw on a pair of jeans, tennis shoes, and an old Polo shirt. There wouldn't be anyone to impress today, so I could be comfortable. I found myself to be pretty horny after looking at the few photos of Truck McPherson that I could find online, but had no prospects to take care of that little problem.

Picking up my cell phone, I held it to my cheek as I thought about what I wanted to do first today. My thinking process didn't take long and I was soon hitting the screen to call Alexander.

"Hi Alexander, it's Nic Netus."

"Hi Nic. Did you make any decisions about the places we were able to see yesterday?"

Alexander had shown me two other theaters after the Madsen, but they were not even close to being what I wanted or needed.

"I did. I am interested in the Madsen, Alexander. I want to send over a contractor today to do an inspection. Is that okay with you?"

"That's excellent news! I'll meet him there. What time?"

"One o'clock would be good." I hesitated and then asked, "Would it be okay if I tagged along with him as well? I'd like to start making some sketches and planning some things out."

"Sure. That would be fine. Bobby going to come again?"

I chuckled into the phone and said, "No, the company that I used is going to send me a replacement this morning. I'm waiting for him now."

Alexander laughed easily and we agreed to talk more this afternoon before I severed the connection. I quickly called the inspector that I had already arranged to help me out and told him to meet me at the theater at one o'clock. Just as I put my cell phone in my pocket, there was a call on the hotel phone.

It was the hotel desk clerk telling me that I had a visitor in the lobby. I informed him that I would be right down.

I met my new bodyguard in the hotel lobby. His name was Wagner and he was a big man—ex-military and no-nonsense. I liked him immediately.

"So, what is the game plan for today, Mr. Netus?" he asked me.

"Please, call me Nic. I thought we would grab some brunch here at the hotel restaurant and then we can go upstairs and fuck, if you want to. We have to be at the theater by one o'clock."

"That is doable, but I will not be available to fuck you while I am on duty, sir."

"You don't have to be so official-sounding about it,

Wagner," I said, needling him.

"I take my job very seriously, sir."

"I see that and am grateful for it. You will keep me safe and I appreciate that. Let's go eat." I turned to walk to the restaurant.

"I will wait and watch from here," Wagner said to me from the entrance to the restaurant.

"You will do what I tell you to do and I'm telling you to join me for brunch. I need to get to know you and vice-versa." We were both big doms—I could tell that in the first few seconds—but I would win this fight since I was paying the bills. Most marked men were seen as submissive, but just like every other sub-group of society, there were more than our fair share of dominants among us.

I could tell that Wagner did not approve of this plan, but I could also see resignation written on his face. I wasn't surprised when he answered, "Yes, sir."

I would bet that he was not used to taking orders from a marked man. He probably had never met a man like me before. I was not intimidated by any man and I had a commanding presence about me that I knew how to use. A lot of men withered in the face of that, but much to Wagner's credit, he held his own in the conversation that occurred while we ate. The other patrons stared at us—probably misreading that Wagner was my Master and I, his Servant.

"You seem pretty comfortable with the amount of attention that you are receiving," he said as we finished eating.

I shrugged my shoulders and said, "I have dealt with it my whole life. But, I'm surprised that you are also comfortable with it."

"I have had quite a few celebrities on my client list before. They draw even more attention than you do."

I smiled, grabbed the check, and said, "I guess I'll have to step up my game. C'mon, let's go to the theater." I liked that he had experience with celebrities because I was planning on drawing a lot of them to my club.

I was itching to go back to the Madsen Theater, like I was being drawn there. I couldn't wait to be back inside it again. I'm not sure that my Uber even came to a complete stop before I bolted out of it and up to the box office doors with Wagner trailing behind me.

"Alexander must already be here," I told Wagner as I pointed at the empty lock box on the ground.

"It looks like your contractor is here also," Wagner said, pointing at a construction van parked across the street.

"Excellent."

We walked inside to find Alexander in the lobby slumped against one of the walls. I hurried to him and gently smacked him on the face while I called his name. There was a cellphone on a charger cord beside him.

"Alexander, Alexander . . ."

He finally came around. "What . . . what happened?"

"Looks like you are doing your best impersonation of Bobby, my bodyguard from yesterday," I said, trying to lighten the mood.

"Tell us what happened," Wagner ordered, getting right to business. He seemed to be on high-alert status.

The realtor turned, saw his cellphone, and seemed to remember. "I was going to charge my phone while I waited on you."

Wagner stooped down to the outlet and ran the tines of the charger over the holes. Sharp blue sparks appeared through the holes of the outlet cover. I immediately appreciated his intellect.

"Looks like it gave you a shock," I told Alexander. "Do you feel like you need to go to the hospital to get checked out?"

"No, no, I'm going to be okay. I just need some fresh air and something to drink. I have something in my car."

"Wagner, can you go with Alexander? Let him sit in his car and watch him for me?"

"But—" he started to protest.

"I'll be fine. This lobby is a dangerous place, but I'm going to go into the theater, sit in one of the chairs, and sketch." I held up my pencils and sketchpad. "I'll be fine."

"Yes, sir. Don't touch anything electrical."

"I have all the lights on already for your inspector," Alexander said as I helped him to his feet.

"Then I won't need to touch anything," I said as I transferred the realtor's slight weight to my husky bodyguard. "I hope you feel better, Alexander. I'll check on you in a little while."

I found a comfy chair on the aisle in the theater and started mapping out my plans for the old girl. I breathed in deeply, but did not detect the cigar smell that I liked from yesterday's visit. All I could smell was dusty furniture and stale air. I couldn't wait to air this place out.

Starting to sketch right away, I could occasionally hear sounds of life and figured it was the contractor banging around. I got up to count the rows of chairs and several times changed my seat, so that I got better angles of the room. I measured multiple times with the tape measure that I had brought with me and documented the numbers in my sketch pad.

After a half hour or so, Wagner came back inside and told me that Alexander had gone home to rest. "He said that he would call you later tonight, boss."

"Thank you, Wagner. Can you do me another favor and get me a coffee from the Starbucks down the street?" I had noticed earlier the familiar green sign as the only other sign of life on this street. "Feel free to get yourself anything you would like also. Save the receipt and I will reimburse you." I was going to have to start carrying cash on me.

"You'll be okay until I return?"

"I will. I feel very safe here."

"Don't leave the theater," he commanded.

Sarcastically, I answered, "Yes, sir."

I was in the middle of sketching the stage area when I got that feeling that people get when someone is watching them.

I quickly looked around, but didn't see anything. Normally, it would have unsettled me, but this time I just shrugged it off as probably the contractor.

That's when I heard it—a very distant musical note, followed by another.

ABOUT THE AUTHOR

Crawford Rhine lives a quiet and happy life in the North of the US, even though he grew up and was educated in the Southern states. While most people flee the other way to warmer weather, Crawford enjoys swimming against the current.

Crawford is easily inspired by travelling. He loves to write while away from home. A trip to Romania and Russia was a dream of a lifetime and where he made lifelong friends. A trip to Denmark over Christmas showed him the power of family and tradition. A trip to Switzerland left hm in total awe of nature and Bohemia confirmed his love for history and its people.

Celebrity and fame inspires Crawford almost daily. He loves to play with the juxtaposition of true masculinity and society's definition of it. It is the opposites that attract him and spur his creativity.

Crawford looks forward to continuing to travel to far-away places and publishing more books in each of his series. He has as many ideas for new books as he does fantastical places on the map to visit.

www.ingramcontent.com/pod-product-compliance
Lightning Source LLC
Chambersburg PA
CBHW070829120626
46556CB00002B/683